HUNTER-SEEKER!

Traveler's jaw dropped open. Behind the panel of safety glass stood a large humanoid figure, at least seven feet tall. Covered with smooth, sleek fur, it walked upright. Its legs were taut and athletic. Its arms were long and limber, terminating in taloned hands. Its face was something out of a nightmare; its eyes fiery red, alert, darting in its hideous lupine face.

The creature pivoted about in its enclosure, large shackles on its ankles.

"At dawn tomorrow," Dr. Stanley said, "armed with a map, your combat knife, and your wits, you will be turned loose in the jungle. I'll give you a four-hour head start."

"And then you release the monster?"

"Yes. Are you game?"

Traveler grimaced. "It seems that I *am* game."

THE TRAVELER SAGA:

FIRST, YOU FIGHT
KINGDOM COME
THE STALKERS
TO KILL A SHADOW
ROAD WAR
BORDER WAR
THE ROAD GHOST
TERMINAL ROAD
THE STALKING TIME
HELL ON EARTH
THE CHILDREN'S CRUSADE

THE PREY

D. B. DRUMM

A DELL BOOK

Published by
Dell Publishing Co., Inc.
1 Dag Hammarskjold Plaza
New York, New York 10017

ISBN: 0-440-16958-5

Printed in the United States of America

September 1987

10 9 8 7 6 5 4 3 2 1

OPM

For Shannon

1

They walked on the beach, relaxed, their voices rising above the crashing of the waves. Laughter. Excitement. The joy of being young. They strolled as if they owned the entire coastline, as if they were the only two people in the world.

He watched them with a slight twinge of envy. They were holding hands and, although he couldn't be sure at this distance, he was sure that their fingers were intertwined. Their progress was slow and leisurely. Occasionally they would bump shoulders in a clumsy, yet graceful motion.

He chewed two aspirin. They left a bitter taste in his mouth. A gentle sea breeze wafted through the lovers' hair. He took a swallow of beer. He glanced at the bottle in his hand. America was on the road to recovery. Hell, they were even brewing beer again. Making new bottles. The beer wasn't half bad, either, although in truth he didn't really remember the taste of prewar beer so he had no real basis for comparison.

He placed the beer on the floor, next to his feet. His eyes lingered for a moment on the Colt .45 strapped to his side. A reminder of who he was, what he was.

The lovers glanced over their shoulders and caught sight of him. They stiffened for a moment. Then the man offered him a friendly wave. He nodded back. The pair continued to walk on the beach, the water lapping at their feet.

A dull ache reverberated in his head. He took the bottle of aspirin and raised it to his lips. In one swift movement he emptied the bottle, washing the tablets down with another swallow of beer. He'd be damned if he'd spend his last time on planet earth buzzed out on prescription painkillers. Aspirin would have to suffice. He waited a few moments for the pain to subside. He realized that, soon, aspirin wouldn't help. Nothing would.

He glanced at the gun at his side. Well, if things got too bad, he could always play target practice with his forehead. He chuckled at the thought. A fine way to end up.

He halfheartedly swatted at a fly buzzing over the bottle. Things could always be worse. He was sure of that. He'd seen it worse. A lot worse.

A sea gull whimpered above him and headed for the waves. The gull swooped down into the sea, making a perfect dive at a passing fish. It came up empty, uttering a frustrated squawk. He studied the gull. It had no beak. Just a gnarled, twisted fist of cartilage protruding from a spot below its eyes.

Mutation, he surmised. There were still some visual

reminders of World War III. You just had to look for them. In this area of the country, well on its way to rehabilitation, there weren't many overt references to the Big Blowout left. At least not the kind you'd noticed straight off. If you peered past the surface layer of things, though, you could spot them.

New generations of animals that didn't look quite right. Plants that had mutated into pale green, sickly things. Flowers that refused to bloom. Soil that refused nourishment to crops. Aberrations of man-spoiled nature begging to be noticed, begging to offer a lesson. Aberrations that were, for the most part, happily ignored.

People, especially Americans, had a tendency to forget bad times quickly, to look forward to the future no matter what.

But he would never forget. Never.

He watched the couple disappear on the horizon. He smiled at their closeness.

Once his life had been filled with people. People he could touch. Laughter he could hear. Tears he could see. Now his world was filled with shadows. Half-distinct glimpses of people, places, events long gone. Memories. He lived on memories. Soon even they would be gone as well.

He took another swig of beer. Yeah, America was picking itself up, pulling itself together these days. It had been over twenty years since the Insanity. He supposed he was glad to see the lawless era come to an end, but he was uneasy about it as well. The new President and Congress were plowing full steam ahead, trying their best to obliterate the horrors of the past.

All human mutations were plucked from cities and towns now, put in remote villages, hidden from view. Areas of the country that couldn't be rehabilitated were bulldozed, erased from view. Cosmetically, things seemed to be getting back to normal. "A Return to Normalcy." That was the popular slogan circulating from state to state. Within a few decades the country would be thriving, at least west of the Mississippi. The northeast section of the country was still far too hot to repopulate. New York. Most of New Jersey. Pennsylvania. Connecticut. They were still nothing more than radioactive rubble. Mass graves for the innocent whose only crime was to live too close to heavily industrialized areas. Accordingly, not too many people spoke of the Northeast anymore. It was as if it had never existed.

His mind flashed back to stories he had heard about Hiroshima following the Second World War. How the Japanese government did its best to do constructional surgery on the area, hoping that by physically forgetting the horror they could psychologically blot it out as well. They managed to do it pretty well. Postnuke America had taken their lead.

Progress was the buzzword again. Education the key. He supposed that was a good, positive goal to pursue but, still, there was this thought hovering in the back of his mind. Wasn't it progress that had plunged the world into the near Total Annihilation in the first place?

The pursuit of the biggest piece of the pie? The need to have the biggest nuclear arsenal? The most powerful bombs? The most affluent society?

The world was passing him by in so many ways. He

was a living, breathing dinosaur, a citizen of a dead era. The Dos Passos-Harper Act made it official last year. Mercenaries were outlawed. They had one of two choices: either join the government officially, on a national, state, or city law-enforcement level, or turn in their guns.

He hadn't been surprised when the President made that move. He'd been expecting it for some time. What did surprise him was how zealously the public had responded to it. Some of the old, hard-line soldiers of fortune who resisted the law found themselves dancing at the end of the rope provided by the smiling proprietor of the local hardware store, a smiling man who flew the flag proudly and displayed a winky, 3-d picture of Jesus in the front of his shop.

A good man. A proud man. A man who prayed fervently for conformity.

Traveler emptied the bottle. There just wasn't room for people like him in America anymore. Since the war he had but one profession. Soldiering. He was a mercenary. A killer. A dispenser of justice. For years he had earned a living fighting for people with the most money or the best cause. Now all that was over. Officially, he was still employed by the government, a "military consultant." He had the papers to prove it. So he got to keep his war toys.

Practically speaking, though, he was definitely out of favor with mainstream society.

He watched the mutant gull make another fruitless pass at the sea. The gull was caught in a dilemma. Its nature compelled it to hunt in one way. Practicality, however, necessitated it find another way to survive. Adapt or die.

Traveler couldn't adapt anymore. He had spent his entire life adapting. Now he was just too tired. He was ready to die. And nature was being very cooperative on that point.

A private jet streaked across the sky. Traveler squinted into the sun. Government plane, most likely. There wasn't enough fuel being processed yet to get the commercial carriers back aloft. It was only a matter of time before the skies were crowded again, though. Progress.

Shortly, life would seem as before. Traveler watched the plane streak over the ocean. Life would never be the same for him, though. Somewhere, in the ashes that were once the East Coast, were the charred remains of his wife and child, obliterated during the first strike.

Nope, he didn't mind dying now. And die he would. The doctor had told him it was just a matter of time.

"How long have you been having these headaches?"

"Four or five months," Traveler had replied.

"Why didn't you come to me sooner?"

Traveler had laughed at that one. "Doc, you have no idea what my poor head has been through in this lifetime." It had been a private joke. The doctor hadn't laughed. He didn't know Traveler's history. Just as well. He wouldn't have believed it.

Just before the Nuke-Out, Traveler and three other buddies had been "accidentally" dosed with an experimental and highly illegal neurotoxin the government was playing around with. He had been a military adviser in El Hiagura, a jerkwater country deemed terribly important by the stammering, senile President of the United States.

Traveler had returned Stateside a basket case, his neural network a mass of tingling explosions. He had found himself overdosing on the world around him. Every whisper seemed like a clap of thunder. The slightest touch stabbed like a knife.

It took him years to get over the aftereffects of the gas. When the headaches had reappeared he figured it was just a small blast from the past, something that would eventually fade away. When the headaches didn't subside he paid a casual call on Sam Nichols, Bay City's G.P.

"It's serious, Mr. Paxton," Nichols had said after taking a series of X rays.

Traveler had been startled to be called by his civilian name. He had come to Bay City a year and a half ago, a wanderer. He wound up siding with a group of kids and ridding the small seaside community of a group of deranged militarists. The mayor of the town, a horse-faced man named Slade, had invited him to stay. The Dos Passos-Harper Act came down and Traveler decided to take him up on the offer.

He was given a house, rent free, outside the city limits and for the past fifteen months had lived, like an aging watchdog, staring at the ocean.

But nobody called him Paxton. For the most part, they didn't call him anything. They were a little uneasy about the presence of this battle-scarred veteran near their picture-perfect pocket of nouveau civilization. They mostly referred to him as "Our Guest." Words spoken as if they were a Haitian voodoo curse.

"Mr. Paxton, you see this area of your brain?"

Traveler had gazed into the blurred X ray. "Yeah?" he replied, not knowing what he was looking at. "This dark area?"

Traveler had sat in the small office and listened patiently. "I could be wrong," Nichols had concluded. "In fact, if you'd care to make a trip to San Francisco, they have CAT scan equipment functioning up there. They'd know for certain. All I have at my disposal are simple X rays."

"I'll take your word for it, Doc." Traveler had smiled leaving his office. "What the hell, nobody lives forever."

Nichols, in his early sixties, nodded. "Who'd want to?"

Traveler removed a cigarette from his pocket and lit up. Not even cancer sticks could hurt him anymore. There was a certain irony to all of this. He had survived for over twenty years living by his wits, his skill at fighting. He had battled roadrats, thugs, insurrectionist armies . . . damn, he had even gone to hell itself, and now he was to be done in by a dark smear on an X ray. Cancer. Inoperable.

Even as he inhaled tiny mutant cells were doing cartwheels through the healthy sections of his brain, infecting them, pummeling them into submission.

He thought for a moment of his long-dead wife and child and smiled. Daddy was coming home. Not in the way he had anticipated, though.

A tingling sensation arose above his eyelids. Instinctively he went for his gun. He glanced to his left and to his right. Nothing on the beach. Yet, there was peril nearby. His brain wasn't fried to the extent that it could invent that feeling.

He removed the Colt from its holster and waited.

He heard a tap-tap-tapping behind him. He turned and walked into the house. Someone was at the front door. Carefully navigating the living room so as not to step on any of the two dozen empty beer bottles, he approached the door.

The knocking continued.

He placed his free hand on the doorknob and jerked the door open suddenly.

Outside, a young man in full army uniform gasped.

Traveler was almost as surprised to see the kid as the kid was to see the gun.

"Lieutenant Kiel Paxton?" the boy squeaked.

"You got him," Traveler replied.

"I was ordered to give you this," the boy said in a near whisper. He extended a trembling hand. Traveler saw the envelope. It had the presidential seal on it.

"Shit," he hissed, holstering his gun and grabbing the envelope. He didn't have to open it to know what it said. It might as well have been a mimeographed note beginning with the word "Greetings."

"Come on in," Traveler said. "Just watch the bottles."

The soldier gulped and carefully entered the house. "My, sir, you have a lot of them."

"Yeah," Traveler said, swatting the palm of his right hand with the still unopened note. "I'm going to build ships in them someday. A new hobby of mine."

He continued to finger the note. He didn't know whether to laugh or punch the infantryman out. It looked as if the government was going to take Traveler out of mothballs. Finally, he began to tear at the envelope. What the hell, no matter how crazy the orders were, he figured it might be better to die on the battlefield than in his sleep.

His concentration was broken by a sudden crash on the rear porch. He and the soldier, guns drawn, ran out the back of the house. The gull with the gnarled beak lay, dead, next to Traveler's chair. Starved to death, Traveler surmised, and just too exhausted to take another swipe at the sea.

The young soldier was stunned. "What . . . what happened?"

Traveler smiled at the young man's fright. "Adapt or die, son," he whispered. "It's still the law of the land."

He pulled out the letter and began to read. The pain in his head subsided.

2

"I don't like that man," Kathy Vega said, shivering slightly as she got into the car.

Daniel Beyers slammed the door after her and walked over to the driver's side of his Volvo, parked near the beach. "Hey," he said, getting into the car. "He got this town out of a real mess last year. We owe him. Besides, he's not going to be around long. Doc Nichols says the guy's got the big C."

Kathy bit her lip, allowing Daniel the last word. Daniel took the gun out of his shoulder holster and placed it in the glove compartment. "Look," he said, trying to placate her. "I'm officially an off-duty cop. Vacation time."

Kathy continued biting her lip. Daniel grimaced, turned the key in the ignition, and sped off. No use trying to reason with her when she was in one of her moods. They'd been together five years. He knew her by now. She'd sulk for almost the entire drive but perk up right before they got to Long Beach.

Lately she'd been pressuring him for a commitment. A ring. A ceremony. He wasn't sure if he was ready for that yet. The last few months or so had been pretty tense. He and Kathy were growing apart. There was nothing he could put his finger on, no real cause. She was involved in running her shop. He worked crazy hours on the force. Perhaps it was only natural that their relationship fritter away. At least that's what he kept trying to tell himself whenever he panicked over the thought of being alone.

They had come together during a hard time, a damned hard time. Now that Bay City was slowly getting back to normal, perhaps it was proper for them to discover that it hadn't been affection that had bound them together for so long, but fear. Fear of the outside world. Fear of the unknown. Fear of facing things without a companion to lean on.

The car sped along the San Diego Freeway south toward Long Beach. Still, he'd give it one more shot. This was the first time he could plan a vacation ever. The first time Southern California had a unified system of law and order. Maybe if they spent a week or so together away from town, away from their separate interests, they'd rediscover each other.

What the hell. Things couldn't get any worse.

From Long Beach they'd take a pleasure boat south to Arrowhead Island, a man-made playland dedicated to drinking, gambling, and fun in the sun.

The Island used to be some sort of floating oil rig off the Mexican coastline. Last year some enterprising guy by the name of Groening decided to spruce it up, build on to it, and cater to the thousands of Southern Californians who were dying to get a taste of hard-core pleasure again.

Daniel smiled to himself. He remembered his grandfather telling him about the great gambling vessels that used to drive the local boys in blue crazy during the 1920s and 1930s. The floating casinos would set up shop beyond the nautical reach of the law and offer booze and every type of gambling imaginable to citizens tired of Prohibition and moral watchdogs.

Every time the law would crack down on them, try to board the boats, the "captains" would simply pull up anchor and move to another, more convenient location.

Maybe that's what Kathy and he needed, a shot of traditional Southern Californian debauchery at a price.

He pulled the car into the parking lot near the Long Beach harbor. Kathy remained mum.

"Well, are you ready for some fun?" he said, overly cheerful.

Kathy nodded. "I suppose."

"Great." He smiled, adding inwardly, This is going to be one fun fucking vacation . . . I bet.

Kathy nearly leapt out of the car. He hesitated for a moment before palming his revolver from the glove compartment. He'd been wearing it for such a long time, he felt incomplete without it.

He removed their bags from the car, locked it, and walked toward the waiting yacht. Kathy walked next to him, silent. Daniel controlled his anger. She was doing everything humanly possible to ruin their trip before it began. Damn. She knew how hard he worked and wheedled to get the chief to allow two consecutive weeks of free time. He was sure the only reason the old man allowed it was that he knew Kathy, liked her, and hoped the pair would work out their problems.

He sighed to himself. Maybe he'd get her drunk tonight and turn on the old charm. That usually worked. If it didn't, he could always jump overboard and swim for home.

They boarded the yacht in silence. Daniel stared out over the white-capped waves. The sun was setting now, a large orange fireball disappearing behind an undulating mass of purple clouds. He took a deep breath of the crisp sea air. At least the weather was cooperating. If Kathy didn't want to relax during their time together, Mother Nature certainly seemed delighted to.

They walked to their stateroom, a smiling bellboy trudging behind them with their bags.

Daniel opened the door to their room with a flourish. Kathy began to enter straightaway. "Wait a minute"—Daniel smiled—"don't you want me to carry you over the threshold?"

"That's only for married people," she replied, marching past him.

Daniel smiled at her retreating back. Fuck me, he thought to himself. He turned to face the bellboy. "I'll take the bags from here."

"Hey, man," the bellboy said, helpfully, "wanna know what I'd do if my old lady acted that way?"

"No," Daniel said, walking away from the tanned young man. "No, I don't."

* * *

Arrowhead Island was all it was cracked up to be. A floating fantasyland of casinos and bars. A place where gaudily dressed (or undressed) showgirls kicked up their heels to the sounds of loud, brassy bands for hours on end and the nightlife lasted until the sun came up.

The place was a three-tiered affair, with the nightlife confined to the bottom rung, the living quarters occupying the second, and the swimming pool-sunning spots placed on the top deck.

It was the perfect place to be.

So why was he having a vacation from hell?

Daniel sat in the bar on the third night of their stay. Kathy sniped at him constantly. It was the same old stuff, really. She wanted a commitment. Soon—as in right now. Daniel tried to explain how he felt. He loved her. He couldn't imagine being with anyone else. But maybe, just maybe, if they stuck it out just a little longer together, tried to weather this new emotional turmoil, he'd feel more confident about saying yes in the near future.

He had nothing against marriage. In fact, he really looked forward to settling down one day. But right now, with both of them trying to cope with the new prosperity, the new sense of normalcy, maybe now wasn't the right time.

She had responded by trying to remove his eyes from their sockets with her fingernails.

And that was on the first night.

Daniel sat alone at his table. Kathy had gone to the ladies' room. Aside from the fact that they were having a miserable time, something more was bothering Daniel. He had the uneasy feeling that the place was being cased. Checked out. He had noticed two burly men in the bar and the casino every night doing nothing more than staring at each and every guest present.

Nothing wrong with that, Daniel surmised. For all he knew, they were Island security. But the cop in him said that they weren't employed by the Island. That they had something else in mind than the well-being of the guests. He had started carrying his gun last night. He wasn't sure why.

For some odd reason it seemed that the two men were concentrating on Kathy and him last night. Tonight, too, for that matter.

He looked at his watch. She'd been gone ten minutes now. He began to worry. Suppose these guys were nothing more than common thieves? Passing along their information to shills outside the casino?

He made a move to leave the table when he saw her. She stood, lounging, at the far end of the bar. She was laughing. God. That was the first time he had seen her laugh in weeks. Drink in hand, dress pulled ever so tantalizingly down over her shoulder, Kathy clinked glasses with two very young, very handsome men.

Daniel gritted his teeth. The barflies were muscular and tanned. Their faces were bereft of lines. Their shirts equally bereft of buttons.

Damn her, he thought. It's not enough she has to treat me miserably . . . she has to flirt not twenty feet away from my table. Daniel tossed a few dollars down on the tabletop and stormed out of the casino.

He took the escalator out of the casino level and stayed on it until he reached the top deck. He marched across the shuffleboard courts to a small bar situated next to the pool. What the hell was going on here, anyway?

He had survived the bad years following the war. He was barely a kid when the Holocaust arrived. He grew up in the ashes of an all-out nuclear war. He had matured, gotten a job on the police force in Bay City. Fought off roadrats. Marauding bikers. Religious nuts. He had gone through every type of hairy time imaginable. Things were better now. Improving every day. So why the hell was his life going down the toilet?

He swallowed a shot of Wild Turkey and stared out into the ocean. The thought of Kathy playing footsie with the two beach bums downstairs caused his hands to tremble. Damn her. Why couldn't she just give him a little more time?

He turned back to the bar. That's when he saw her. She was young, barely out of her teens, with almond-colored skin and long, flowing black hair. She wore a saronglike dress, cinched tightly in front of her breasts. Her eyes were large, hazel-colored. Her lips were moist and pale.

He blinked his eyes, amazed at how much he took in in just a few brief seconds.

The woman looked up at him and smiled.

He smiled back.

What the hell, he thought, thinking of Kathy downstairs. Two can play the flirting game. He walked over to her, still smiling. "Hi," he offered.

"Hello," she replied. Her voice had a nice lilt to it. "What is that you're drinking?" She put strange accents on her syllables, giving them a soothing, singsongish quality.

"Wild Turkey," he said.

"For a wild man?" she asked.

Oh, brother. Something totally adolescent stirred within him. This would be a dream come true for any red-blooded guy in the world. "I've been called that and worse," he said, amazed at how lame the words sounded as soon as they left his mouth. Man, if she bought that line, he could probably sell her swampland in Florida.

She looked into his eyes and laughed. Softly. Gently. Exposing a set of sparkling teeth. "Tonight, you will be my wild man."

"Oh, I will, will I?" He was smiling stiffly now. Everything he said sounded dumb. Dumb. Dumb. Yet the woman kept smiling. This had to be a dream.

"Yes," she said, taking him by the arm. "And tonight I will tame you."

She took the drink from his hand and placed it on the bar. Without a word she led him to the escalator descending to the living quarters. Daniel offered no resistance. He moved as if he were walking on air.

He wanted to pinch himself. There he was, in the middle of the sultry Pacific, jilted by his girlfriend and, moments later, picked up by one of the most beautiful women he had ever seen in his life. Things were definitely looking up.

The woman led him to a cabin at the end of a dimly lit corridor. She placed a key in the lock and turned it swiftly. He heard the lock click. She swung open the door. "Enter, my wild man." She smiled.

Daniel eagerly did as he was told. He heard the *thwack* before he felt the prick of pain at the base of his skull. He felt his head swing from side to side as he tried to maneuver his body around to face the girl in the doorway. His legs were numb already. The cop in him told him that he had been hit by a supertranquilizer.

His hand instinctively went for the gun in his shoulder holster. His arm didn't have the strength to propel his hand that far up. Instead, he wound up pawing his stomach as his body began to lurch forward.

"What the fuck," he mumbled, watching the floor rise up to greet his forehead. He was unconscious before he hit the ground.

When he awoke he found himself in a room resembling a greenhouse. He was handcuffed to a chair. He took a deep breath. The air was hot and moist. He knew he was no longer on Arrowhead Island.

He heard a whimpering noise arising from nearby. He tried to shake his head clear. His vision was still slightly blurred. He blinked his eyes several times, trying to focus. He turned his head as far as he could without losing his balance.

Kathy was bound and gagged in a corner of the room. Her dress was torn and soiled. Her arms and legs were wrapped around a pole of some sort. She had been beaten. He could see that, even in the murky light of the greenhouse.

Instinctively he tried to reach her. He strained against the back of the chair. He felt the legs of the chair slip out from under him. In an instant he and the chair were sprawled on the ground. He struggled, growling, against the cuffs. They dug deep into his flesh.

"Good, good," came a voice. "You have spirit. I like that."

Daniel, his face flattened against the floor, glanced

to his right. A pair of scuffed black shoes was positioned directly against his nose.

"Now, Officer Beyers, you seem to be a man in good physical shape. Let us make a deal, you and I. If you will help me, I will allow your pretty young friend to go free. If you don't cooperate, I will provide her with a very slow and painful death. And you, Officer Beyers, will get to watch the entire spectacle."

Daniel heard Kathy whimper in the background. Tears of rage and frustration welled up in his eyes. He struggled against the handcuffs digging into his wrists.

Abruptly he stopped struggling and allowed the tears to flow.

Sometimes it just didn't pay to take a vacation.

3

Traveler had never liked Las Vegas. His parents had taken him there briefly when he was a kid. Maybe ten, eleven years old. His dad worked like a dog all year and then, as a big incentive, was given two whole weeks off in the middle of the summer. The Old Man based his entire year around those two weeks. For those fourteen days he was the Man of the House, an adventurer ready to lead his family on leisurely bouts with nature.

For the most part, they always wound up going someplace along the Jersey Shore. Seaside Heights. Lavalette. West Point Island. Small, sluggish bergs where potbellied dads, middle-aged moms, and braces-encased teenagers with hormones bursting could pretend to be exotic for a short period of time.

This one year, though, the Old Man had won a lottery in a bowling alley. Had a couple of hundred dollars extra. That year they were going to have a real adventure. They were Going West. Young Traveler's mind had reeled at the thought. West. His mind had pictured some of the great natural resources he associated with that area: Yellowstone Park, the Grand Canyon, Disneyland.

Instead, the Old Man had opted for Vegas. Traveler remembered his disappointment as his father angled their station wagon into the place. The town looked like a parking lot. It was hot and dusty, bleak and barren. In the harsh light of day the mammoth casinos looked like the tacky joints they really were. Without the aid of countless blinking lights and money-hungry crowds, the gambling establishments looked like Brobdingnagian porn houses lifted from the dregs of Times Square.

The Old Man, though, had been mesmerized by the sight. He had worked his entire life to visit a fantasyland like this. Traveler's parents took to the casinos at night. Hell, they even managed to win a hundred bucks or so during the vacation, playing the slot machines.

But for young Traveler the experience had been a brief jaunt into hell. It was a place filled with polyester, cigarette smoke, bad breath, and looks of desperation.

Vegas was now the capital of the United States. Not officially, of course. New Washington was located some one hundred feet away from the city limits, a series of hastily constructed military buildings that had been embellished architecturally over the past ten years.

But, staring out from the New White House, Traveler could see the casinos again, miraculously intact.

During the course of the last ten years they had actually reopened. Now, with a haphazard sort of peace in place throughout the country and gasoline in plentiful supply once again, crowds were making their way back to this monetary mecca.

Parents brought their kids. He could imagine the fathers' spiel: "Hell. It'll be educational. We can see where the President lives!" Dad could also get a peek at the long-legged chorines who still bumped and gyrated on the light-bulb-littered runways as well.

Traveler fidgeted in his straight-back chair. He placed a forefinger beneath the collar of his shirt and tried to pry it loose. He hated wearing suits. He saw no reason why he had to wear one now.

Idiocy. Traveler fingered his tie as if it were a small boa constrictor bent on crushing his windpipe. David Orwell walked into the room. Traveler rolled his eyes. He should have known. Orwell had been with Traveler in El Hiagura, one of the four lucky individuals to have been dosed with the neurotoxin. Three of them still lived. Orwell had done the best, snaring a job with the new government, getting out of the merc trade before the new law kicked in.

"Don't you look bureaucratic," Orwell cracked.

"Why the hell do I have to wear this monkey suit?" Traveler groused. "I'm just going to see Jefferson."

"He's the President now."

"He was the President two years ago too. He was still wearing blue jeans then."

"Things have changed, Kiel," Orwell explained softly, sitting down in a chair next to Traveler. "Jefferson is trying to bring the government back to where it was before the war. That involves the respect of the people. A little pomp. A little ceremony."

"I remember Jefferson when he was a roadrat beheading babies," Traveler said, leaving his tie at peace. "Dress was casual back then."

Orwell sighed and shook his head. Traveler stared at the man and wondered if he had headaches as well. A sudden stab of pain sliced into his forehead. Traveler reached into the pocket of his ill-fitting suit and produced a vial of aspirin. He popped four.

"Feeling bad?" Orwell asked.

"Catching a cold," Traveler replied.

"Well, Louise picked out a nice suit for you anyway."

"Louise is a Nazi," Traveler said. "She *made* me wear this thing . . . on your orders."

Orwell shrugged. "She's a nice girl. A damned good secretary."

Traveler stared at the man across from him. "Are we from the same planet or what? We were soldiers together. Mercs together. What the hell has gotten into you?"

Orwell offered a condescending smile. "Progress, Kiel. We're moving ahead. We have to change with the times. Come on. Jefferson is waiting."

"Well, I'd hate to keep His Highness from the job of governing America," Traveler said, getting to his feet. "He probably has a lot of papers to push this afternoon . . . or does he have a Louise to push them for him?"

"Bad attitude, Kiel."

"Bad move making me dress up like an accountant, Orwell."

The two men walked into the next room. Behind a desk the size of an aircraft carrier sat the equally imposing form of President John Marchmont Jefferson, former roadrat, born again patriot, and, up until a year or so ago, 100 percent good ole boy. The President beamed as Traveler walked into the room.

He stood, extending a massive hand in Traveler's direction. "Glad to see you, Traveler," boomed a voice from beneath a neatly cropped beard.

"Good to see you, Mr. President," Traveler said, allowing his hand to be engulfed by the neatly manicured paw.

"Sit down. Sit down," Jefferson said. "Both of you."

Traveler took a seat in a Naugahyde chair before the President. Orwell sat at his side.

"How are they treating you in Bay City?" Jefferson asked.

"Politely. Like a leper."

Jefferson nodded, understandingly. "I told the mayor there to make you feel right at home."

"He has. But since Dos Passos-Harper, the citizens don't exactly welcome a mercenary in their midst. Even a retired one."

"Yes, I'm sure they're a little skittish," the President replied, "but Dos Passos-Harper was necessary. The times are changing, Traveler."

Traveler sighed. He was about to become the recipient of The Speech. He had heard variations of The Speech ever since he was a kid. From the Old Man. From his teacher. From the top brass in the Army. He awaited it now with a morbid sense of anticipation. He hadn't heard it since before the Big Nuke-Out. He wondered how it had evolved over the years.

Jefferson took a deep breath. "America today is probably the strongest country in this postnuclear world. We have realigned the remnants of thirty states. We have unified government again on national, state, and local levels. We've reopened some of the major freeways, guaranteeing safe passage for our citizens. We have a standing Army. Navy. And we're actually getting an Air Force together."

Jefferson paused, waiting for Traveler to make a comment. The only thing Traveler could muster was a feeble, "Neat."

Jefferson ignored it. "And this past year we discovered a cache of MX missiles, left intact after the first strike."

Traveler blinked, astounded.

The President grinned. "Yes, we now have nuclear capability for the first time in over twenty years."

"That's crazy!" Traveler stated. "You, of all people, should know what the country was like after the Nuke-Out. Why the hell would you restore the MX arsenal? Destroy the fuckers."

Jefferson frowned. "Now, Traveler, don't get riled up. We don't mean to use the MX's offensively. They're a deterrent. That's all."

"Oh, right." Traveler nodded.

Orwell shot him a withering look. Traveler returned his glance, forming a here-we-go-again expression with his face.

Jefferson leaned forward in his oversized chair. "Traveler, we have managed, thanks in part to you, to secure all our borders. For the first time since the war, our citizenry is safe. Bandits. Thugs. Street scum. They're things of the past. The first time someone shows a bad streak—*wham*—we have them off the streets and into the slammer."

Traveler wanted to mention the internment camps for the poor unfortunates born mutated thanks to the nuclear deterrents of two decades ago, but he felt it wouldn't be a judicious move.

"But," Jefferson continued, "we're still having problems."

"And that's where I come in," Traveler said.

"Hopefully, yes," Jefferson replied.

"What kind of problems?"

"We're not sure. Orwell? Why don't you fill him in?"

Orwell took a file folder from a small table nearby. "There are rumors of scientific experiments being conducted somewhere near the Southern California border," he began. "We've attempted to instigate military sweep searches of the area but they've been spotty. Frankly, we don't know where to begin."

"Scientific experiments," Traveler repeated. "Of what nature?"

"We've drawn a blank there too," Orwell answered.

"So, for all you know some guy in an adobe hut may be trying to come up with the formula for the better M & M's," Traveler shrugged.

"Can it, Kiel," Orwell snapped. "This is some serious shit here. There are rumors circulating that someone, an independent operator, is trying to develop a weapon that would totally alter conventional warfare. You remember the last time someone tried that, right?"

Traveler ran his left hand over his forehead. "Yeah.

Only that time it was our own government playing with our heads."

"We have no idea what form these experiments are taking," Orwell continued. "But we know where our friend is getting his guinea pigs from."

He removed a large eight-by-ten photo and tossed it Traveler's way. Traveler ensnared it with his left hand. He looked at it.

Orwell continued, "That's Arrowhead Island. It's a floating pleasure palace situated in the Pacific on the Mexican-California border. During the past six months forty vacationers have vanished from the place."

"Shouldn't be hard to trace them," Traveler said. "Just send a couple of men down there."

"We did. They disappeared as well."

"What about the owner of the place?"

"A guy named Groening. Arthur. He's clean. He's as upset as we are about the disappearances. He's afraid the publicity will be bad for his establishment."

"Too bad. Any of the victims ever show up again?"

"We found a few body parts off the coast. That's about it."

"Sounds like you have a problem."

"It gets better. Except for our men, all of the victims have been couples. Young, usually. One minute they're on board, the next . . . gone."

Traveler nodded. "So, basically, what you're telling me is that you have a gambling joint making people disappear and that, somehow, you've linked those disappearances up with a *rumor* that some nutcase is developing a superweapon."

"It's more than a rumor, Traveler," Jefferson said,

tossing Traveler a file folder. Traveler opened it. There were photos of two half-mauled male bodies. From the remains, Traveler could see that they had been efficiently and systematically tortured before having the tops of their heads blown off.

"The chemicals used to make those burns have been off the market for years. They were never used in pharmaceutical pursuits," Jefferson said. "They were used, primarily, for military experimentation. There are traces of radiation there as well."

Traveler closed the folder and placed it on the President's desk.

"So," he sighed. "What do you want me to do?"

Jefferson beamed and reached into his top drawer. He produced a small billfold and, standing, reached over to hand it to Traveler. "Open it."

Traveler did so. There was a badge and a small document inside. Traveler's eyes nearly bugged out of his head. "Central Intelligence Agency?"

Jefferson nodded proudly. "Yup. We've restarted the Agency. The last time we talked, it was pretty lightweight stuff. Right now, it's still pretty small. But in time we hope to have it back on track again, one hundred percent. You know, we even have a national computer data bank now?"

Traveler gaped at the shield. A mixture of anger and shock roared through his body. "The CIA . . . awww jeez."

"It'll be a different kind of CIA," Orwell injected. "I mean this time we're the good guys."

"Uh-huh," was all Traveler could think of.

Jefferson ignored Traveler's mixed feelings. "What we'd like you to do is to go down to Arrowhead Island undercover. Since most people know you as Traveler, you can even use your real name. No one will suspect a thing. You won't be able to take the Meat Wagon with you or most of your toys. This time out, you're going to have to look like Joe Average. Nice suit, by the way."

"Thank Louise," Traveler said numbly.

"Basically, we want you to go down there as bait," Jefferson continued. "Make yourself very available to whomever is doing the snatching. Play into their hands. Find out what's going on. Get yourself out of there in one piece and leave the rest to us."

"Is that all?" Traveler asked, blinking.

"You're the only man who could pull something like that off," the President concluded.

Traveler still stared at the billfold. "And if I say no?"

"Well, then I'm afraid we must enforce the Dos Passos-Harper Act. You'll either have to join up with some sort of government law-enforcement agency or give up all your weaponry."

Traveler glared at Jefferson.

The President smiled. "And live the rest of your life staring at the sea. Of course we'd have to take back your privileges in Bay City too. But I'm sure you'll fit in with the work force. Maybe get a gig in a bank or something."

Traveler thought that over for a moment. He knew he didn't have a lot of time left to live . . . but scrounging for a living for your last months . . . he'd go crazy. Either that or he'd be tempted to put a bullet through his head. He fingered a deep red gash on his forehead. He had tried that once. He couldn't even get that right. He stared at the President.

"You *still* suck," Traveler said evenly.

"It's good to know that power hasn't turned my head around," Jefferson said, tossing in a wink for good measure.

"Look," Traveler said. "I hate the CIA, all right? They were always shitheads. They have a tradition of being shitheads. They were anti-anything that wasn't CIA-instigated."

"It's a whole new ball game," Jefferson insisted.

"Maybe," Traveler countered. "But even if it is, your plan has enough holes to drive a semi through."

"Such as?" Jefferson asked.

"You sent two guys down there already, right? They came back looking like relief maps of Peru. Now you're willing to send me down there. Whoever it is making off with the tourist trade is going to spot me a mile off. You said yourself that just about all of the victims have been couples. I'm a widower. No wife. And no wifey, no takee."

Jefferson smiled in silence. He glanced at Orwell. Orwell coughed nervously, got to his feet, and walked to the door of the room. He opened the door and led in a young, blond-haired woman.

Orwell coughed a second time. "Uh, Kiel, I'd like you to meet operative Michelle Trinen."

"Who," Jefferson added, "for all intents and purposes will be known, from this day forward, as Mrs. Kiel Paxton."

Traveler felt his stomach turn. "Awww, jeez."

Jefferson's booming laughter filled the room "Gotcha," he bellowed.

Traveler rubbed his forehead. It hurt. A lot.

4

He sat in his hotel room, his head swimming, a half-drained bottle of tequila at his side. He took a long drag off his cigarette. He glanced at the smoking stick of tobacco in his hand. Smoking was a new habit. Stupid. He knew it wasn't a real health plus, but he didn't really care anymore. About anything.

He stared out the window at the great expanse of Nevada desert before him. If government policies continued to slog ever onward, it would only be a matter of time before someone came up with the technology to begin underground testing of new and improved nuclear weapons again soon.

He imagined what it would be like to feel the ground rumbling beneath his feet. The radiation would be ventilated "safely" of course, just the way it had been in the 1950s and 1960s, when clouds of officially sanctioned radiation drifted out of Nevada as far as upper

New York State, causing death and destruction for cattlemen and farmers . . . and ordinary citizens who, the day of tests, scraped fallout off their cars as if it were a light dusting of snow.

Of course the government never actually *told* anyone about the dangerous levels of radiation. Even when cancer began blossoming in the parents, in the young, the agencies involved stonewalled it. For what? Eventually to have the capability to destroy civilization.

Which they did.

He took a swig from the bottle. No one ever seemed to learn from past mistakes in this world. The liquor went down hard, leaving a stinging taste in his mouth.

He reached down and grabbed a cookie from a tray. Room service was back. He regarded the chocolate-sandwich biscuit in his hand before replacing it. He remembered having Oreos as a kid. Loving them. When Kiel, Jr., was about two years old, he went out and got a jumbo box of the treats for the tot. The kid hated them. Smart kid. A month or so later he found out that most of the creamy filling wasn't cream at all. Lard. Beef extract. Fat. He tossed the cookies and a lot of childhood memories down the kitchen disposal unit the very same day.

He gazed deep into the desert and felt a twinge of sadness. He was losing control. Again. He remembered how it was before the war. He was in high school when he suddenly felt it. "I have no control," the young student realized one day. In his young lifetime he had witnessed political assassinations, illegal wars, governmental scandals, man-made gas shortages, religious wars, and capricious exercises in terrorism. On that day in high school one of his best friends was hit and killed by a respectable member of the town council who had been 100 percent juiced while behind the wheel. He, young Kiel Paxton, could do nothing about the death. He could do nothing to right the wrong. All he could do was to go home, overwhelmed, fritter over a geometry book, and wonder about the senselessness of it all. At the tender age of sixteen he rationalized that he would spend his entire life spinning wildly in a world that was dedicated to usurping power from the individual. Surely he *had* to be wrong.

Traveler flicked the ashes off the end of his cigarette. He had been right, of course. Before the war the ordinary citizen, the guy in the street, had no control of his life.

Certain truths were kept from him. Back then no one really had any idea of what the government was doing with tax-paid dollars. You never really knew if the new car you bought was a death trap or not. If the land your house was built on was the sight of a toxic dump way back when. If the air you breathed was healthy. If the food you ate contained cancer-causing chemicals. You spent your entire life living in the dark.

Maybe, in a very perverse way, that's why Traveler had excelled in combat. At least, in a conventional warfare situation, you took responsibility for your own life. You knew exactly what was going on. Someone shot at you. If you were smart, if you were lucky, if you were good, you killed the other guy before he killed you. That was it. Plain and simple. Events happened so quickly, the backdrop changed so suddenly, that you had no time to hesitate. No time to defer to laws, to red tape, to trends. You either lived or you died. That was that.

In civilian life, however, you were always at the mercy of something or someone bigger than you. A President who wanted to make the history books. A company that wanted to make a bigger profit. A Bible thumper who wanted you to convert to the true religion at the expense of the millions of unbelievers who hadn't seen the light as yet.

He watched the sun set behind the distant hills. Stars began to emerge. He experienced a vast wave of melancholy. Hopefully, somewhere out there, things were different, better, in some unknown world, on some undiscovered planet.

He smiled to himself. He remembered himself as a kid, wanting to go into space. He had watched enough *Star Trek* reruns to qualify as a futurist. He had read enough wondrous stories by Ray Bradbury. Seen enough vintage science-fiction films. He had dreamed of being one of the first on an orbiting space station. Of being an astronaut.

Then, in '86, there had been the Challenger tragedy. Seven visionaries, seven lives snuffed out. The reason? Bureaucracy. Someone had wanted to save some money, save some time, make a buck, take a shortcut.

Seven souls, overwhelmed by the idiocy around them, not even being allowed the privilege of controlling their own adventure into space.

He drained the bottle in one gulp. His stomach churned, rebelling against the urine-colored liquid. As much as he had hated his wanderings in the decades since the Big Blowout, he had savored the control factor. For better or for worse, and most often it was decidedly for the worse, he had been in control of his own life. He had triumphed or failed solely on his own initiative. He had a code of morality and he had tried to live up to it.

But now civilization was once again taking the reins. He glanced at his right hand. The cigarette had burned down to his fingertips. He hadn't registered the pain. He tossed the smoldering butt out the window.

Yeah. He was losing control. Again. Hell, and now he was going to die because of some fast-moving growth in his brain. He didn't even know the scientific name for it. Or the cause. He didn't know why. He didn't know how. He didn't even know when. He lit another cigarette. Yup, he was feeling like a real American now. Proudly impotent.

He flicked on the radio next to his bed. Moe Bandy was singing a prewar tune: "I can tell by the way she's all over him that she's all over me."

A sudden buzzing drowned out the radio. His head was throbbing now. He turned off the radio and pulled his .45 from the holster slung over his headboard. He trained it on the door to the room.

A knock reverberated through the silence.

"Come in," he said gently.

The door swung open. Michelle Trinen entered. Pretty. No doubt superintelligent. After all, she was a CIA operative. He gazed at her open mouth as she caught sight of the gun. He disregarded the small gasp that came from it, concentrating instead on her features. Deep blue eyes. Round face. Nice cheekbones.

She was very attractive. She'd be even more so in her mid-thirties. If she lived that long.

He slowly lowered the gun. "Want a drink?"

She ignored the offer and pulled up a chair next to his bed. "Why did you walk out of the meeting?"

He unscrewed the cap on a new bottle. "Why do you think?"

"You don't want to work with me," she surmised.

"No, I don't," he said. "But don't flatter yourself. It's not you. It's not because you're a woman. I'm not a misogynist."

"Then what's your problem?"

He tipped the top of the bottle toward the open window. "Out there. That's the problem. The *world's* the problem."

Michelle smiled. "They didn't tell me you were a philosopher."

"They probably didn't tell you a lot about me. But I suppose you think you know all there is to know about my history," Traveler said, taking a sip.

She flashed him an icy stare. "Name, Kiel Paxton. Height, five feet eight inches. Eyes, blue. Hair, brown. Born, June 6, 1964. Place of birth, Elizabeth, New Jersey. Shall I go on?"

"You know data," Traveler replied evenly. "Data doesn't mean shit." He gave her a small smirk. "A little tidbit I picked up before the war."

"Look," she said, "I don't know what your problem is and I don't have the time or the inclination to worry about it. We start tomorrow."

Traveler sat up in the bed. "Oh, we do? Well, Ms. CIA Agent, what's our plan of attack?"

Michelle shrugged. "We go down there heavily

armed. Colt 9-mm assault carbines, maybe. Beretta military 9-mm auto pistols. Paws ZZ7 .45 sub gun."

Traveler nodded. He smiled encouragingly. "Wrong," he said flatly.

The woman was startled. Traveler continued, "We go down with almost no weaponry. We drive down in the worst piece-of-shit car we can find and board the pleasure barge as Mr. and Mrs. Joe Average. If we get through this, and I'm not sure at all we will, we get through on brainpower, not firepower."

"That's ridiculous."

"How long have you been an agent, Ms. Trinen?"

"Two years."

"Field or office work?"

"Office mostly"—she bristled—"but I'm damned good on a firing range and my tactical-planning-class scores are—"

"I'm sure you're aces when it comes to theory," Traveler said dully. "But we're talking fieldwork here."

"I realize that."

"You do? There's a very big difference between drilling a cardboard target and drilling a human being."

The woman glared at him. Traveler stood and gazed out the window. "When a slug hits a human being," he said, "it doesn't make such a nice round hole. The hole at the point of impact may be small, but the exit point is usually big, round, ragged. Bits of tissue and bone tend to scatter. If you're lucky, your victim dies from a single shot. But usually you're not lucky. Usually you're firing a semiautomatic at the very least.

"So your target gets hit more than once. Five times.

Ten times. If you're close up, you hear the sounds the bullets make when they tear into his flesh. *Thwap. Thwap. Thwap.* You watch his eyes as they register surprise. You see the body spin. The hands claw the air trying to grab on to something, anything, that will break the fall, undo the wounds.

"You watch the legs buckle. Blood is all around now. He's gasping. He's pissing in his pants. Maybe he's moaning. No, it's not a moan. It's smaller than a moan. A sickening little whine, almost like a baby's cry. Then he hits the ground. His body shakes. Quivers. He thrashes about spasmodically. Maybe for a terribly long second or two. Maybe for a minute. And all the time he's whining. Gasping. Gurgling."

He turned from the window and faced her. "And *that,* my dear Ms. CIA Agent, is only one target. And that, Ms. CIA Agent, is considered a clean kill. Maybe, someday, I'll tell you about the messy stuff."

He watched the woman stand. "So you've killed and I haven't. Does that make you any better than me?"

Traveler shook his head sadly. "No. You don't get it, do you? It's not *fun.* It's not anything to be proud of. Sometimes it's something you *have* to do to stay alive. *You* don't have to do this. That geek, if he even exists, in Mexico isn't threatening your life."

"You want me to just up and quit?" the woman asked, incredulously.

"If you have any sense, yes. Stay behind a desk. Stay simple. Stay happy. Death is complicated."

"Oh, give me a break," she said, seething. "I don't need a lecture on death. I've never killed anybody, true. But I've seen a lot of people die. Slowly. Painfully. Most of them radiation victims. I was a kid when the bombs came down, Paxton. I grew up in a town that spent most of its time defending itself from roadrats. The rest of the time was spent preparing itself for defense.

"The country has changed since then. I don't want to see it torn down again. If this . . . geek . . . as you call him, is a threat to our stability, I *want* to stop him. I *want* to be down there."

Traveler nodded. "How the hell are you going to stop him when you've never experienced combat?"

"How the hell am I going to experience combat if I have old farts like you telling me to stay safe and pure? No, you're not upset that I'm a woman . . . you're offended. I can spot your kind a mile away. A kindly, open-minded sort of guy who really and truly believes that women are equal to men but thinks that they'd be happiest if they stayed home and took care of the kids and had three meals on the table for Mr. Right."

Traveler shrugged. "Think what you want. We have to work together. We don't have to like each other. All I'm telling you is that killing is serious business. It's not all it's cracked up to be."

"And you hate it, right?" the woman asked.

"No," Traveler said sadly. "No. You actually get to like it. You enjoy the him-or-me angle. You get a high from it, a surge of adrenaline that can't be matched by anything. Not drugs. Not sex. Not anything. And, adding to the high, is the knowledge that you're fighting for the good guys, the right side. That makes it legal. So you find more bad guys to hunt down. *Bang. Bang. Bang.* You kill some more. And then some more. You come home and your bosses give you a medal and a bigger gun. Then you're sent off hunting again.

"And you find that you're getting good at it. Damn good. You're enjoying it more. Earning a reputation. Respect, even. Before you know it, you're addicted to killing, Miss Agent. You're addicted mentally. Physically. When you don't have a gun in your hand, you feel naked. When you're not in a life and death situation, you feel hollow. Incomplete."

He grabbed the headboard of his bed and squeezed it tight with both hands, white-knuckling it. "You want to hear something sick? For the last year I've been sitting in one of the most beautiful spots I've ever seen in my life. Everything was perfect. The sky was nice. The people were nice. Life was nice. And do you know what? I was bored. Because of the Dos Passos-Harper act, I wasn't allowed to kill. I was asked to do the unthinkable. Live like a normal human being.

"Personally, I think this whole mission sucks. I think it's half-assed and wrongheaded. I think the way this country is heading stinks. But I'm taking the assignment, and do you know why?"

The woman stared at him silently. Traveler almost growled at her. "Because I'm a junkie. I'm a killing machine. That's what I do best. And, like some ghetto hophead, I'm jumping at the chance to go into a fucked-up situation where I can expect anything and, hopefully, will kill a few people."

He released the headboard and glared at her angrily. "The kind of guy I am, lady, is the kind of guy who isn't crazy about seeing a real-live, normal human being get sucked into that kind of addiction. I'm the kind of guy who looks at you and sees something valuable, something *clean.*

"You want to go down there with me, fine. I can't

stop you. But once the shooting starts, once the blood begins to flow, you can't put away the gun and you can't wash the blood out of your dreams. Ever."

He flopped back down onto the bed, propping his head up on a pillow. Michelle pushed the chair away from the bed. "Are you finished?"

"Yeah," Traveler sighed. "I'm finished all right."

"Fine," the woman said. "I'm an early riser. I'll expect to see you at the armament center at 9 A.M. We can pick our weapons, then go to the garage and select a car. We should be on the road by eleven."

She turned and walked toward the door. Traveler called to her before she left the room. "Miss Trinen?"

"What?"

He watched her grasp the doorknob tightly. "How old are you?"

"Twenty-four."

Traveler cradled the bottle of tequila in the crook of his left arm. "Twenty-four," he mused. She edged out of the room. "Miss Trinen?" he called.

"What?"

"You don't know shit," he said, smiling.

He raised the bottle to his lips as the door slammed. He leaned over and turned the radio back on. Moe Bandy wasn't singing anymore. Moe Bandy hadn't sung in years.

Traveler left the radio on.

The room was filled with the sound of static.

5

The afternoon sun beat down on the roof of the Subaru as it zipped along the Arizona border.

"This is the most inconspicuous car you could come up with?" Traveler asked, behind the wheel.

The woman next to him stared at the passing terrain. "I picked one that could run, all right? Is that a crime?"

Traveler sighed. "No. No crime." The car was an '84 two-door automatic with four-wheel drive. The dash looked like an outtake from a George Lucas film. Traveler hated to admit it, but it had been a good choice.

That morning, from the armament center, he had pulled out a Remington 870 twelve-gauge riot shotgun, a weapon he was used to wielding. He also managed to ensnare an Amate AR-180 light assault rifle. He'd been using one for years.

He didn't know why he picked them up. They'd be

useless once they arrived at the boat. He figured that, since the abductions had started, security on board would be pretty tight. He'd have to tough it out with his combat knife and the ninja shuriken he kept tucked in a wristband if things got really hairy. The guns would, more than likely, remain in the trunk. For good measure this morning, he had also picked up a pound or so of plastique. He had no idea why, since the car was open and vulnerable to attack, but he felt easier knowing that, with the plastique aboard, if anyone tried to blow them away, they'd wind up blowing themselves off the planet as well.

"Let's make sure we get our stories straight," Traveler said. "Go through it one more time."

"Why don't I just tattoo it on my thigh?" the woman asked.

"Because if you forget it and you have to check your notes, you'll get us arrested for lewd behavior."

Michelle sighed. "Fine. You are Kiel Paxton. You own a hardware store in Vegas. I'm Mrs. Kiel Paxton. We met cute three years ago. I went into your store looking for a plumber's helper and you said that was you."

"I have a great sense of humor," Traveler grumbled.

"Hey, I didn't come up with this story. Thank your pal Orwell."

"He's no pal of mine anymore."

"We got married six months later. I'm a librarian. We have a lovely little tract house on the city limits. We're madly in love but we can't have children because the last war put the kabosh on your sperm count."

"I'll kill Orwell when I get back."

For the first time in the last twenty-four hours, Michelle found herself smiling. "Oh, I don't know. It sounds pretty plausible to me."

Traveler grimaced and drove in silence. Michelle glanced at him. "Do you feel funny about this?"

"Funny?"

"About me posing as your wife?"

Traveler flashed a look in Michelle's direction. The afternoon light was pouring through the sunroof, enveloping her short blond hair in a sort of halo. "No. I imagine I could do worse."

"Thanks. That's not what I meant."

"Oh." Traveler nodded. "You mean because I had a wife once."

"Uh-huh."

Traveler thought about that a moment. He glanced at the wedding ring issued to him by the government. He hadn't worn one in over twenty years. "Ancient history," he answered.

"Uh-huh."

"Hell, when I got married . . . well, you weren't even born yet."

"What was she like?"

Traveler gripped the wheel tightly. Right now, en route to their rendezvous point, he couldn't even remember her face. That thought caused a momentary surge of anger. He relaxed somewhat after a few seconds. She'd understand. If she knew the hell he'd gone through since . . .

He shrugged. "She was the best. Her name was Roberta. Roberta Lilith Toland. I met her in high school."

"High school sweethearts?"

"Not at first." He smiled, his wife's face slowly forming in his mind. "She hated my guts. I was from the wrong side of the tracks, you see. I didn't have any big dreams of going to college, becoming a businessman and conquering the world. I pretty much supported my mom from the time I was old enough to work."

"What about your dad?"

"He died when I was twelve. Great guy. Factory worker. Had the guts to try to stop a holdup in an A & P. Didn't have the moves, though. The robber shot him, point-blank, with a shotgun."

"They ever catch the guy?"

"Uh-huh. It was a girl. My age. Twelve. Cuban kid. Knew about six words of English."

He stood on the gas, lighting the "turbo" light on the dash. "Life is filled with its little ironies, isn't it?"

"I suppose," Michelle answered, affecting a detached attitude.

Traveler saw a town looming in the distance. "Tell me something, Ms. Agent. Why the heck are you so hopped up about serving in the CIA?"

Michelle stared at the road ahead. "I don't know. I just feel I have to. After the war things were pretty rough in Nevada. It was a regular Wild West Show. My dad had been a lawyer. After the war he tried his best to handle manual labor. My mother, with her garden, managed to keep us going for years. We were pretty lucky. Our town came through it pretty much intact. We all pulled together. The adults made sure the children were educated, tried to stress a sense of morality.

"There was a library of videos in town, so all of us kids got the chance to see what the world was like before the Big Blast. I suppose we all grew up wanting to shove the world back in that direction. This is my big chance, I guess."

Traveler nodded. He couldn't argue with that. In a way that was why he joined the service. He wanted to make the world a better place. He couldn't tell her that she was as wrong as he had been.

"You're the weirdest soldier I ever met," she said.

He cracked a smile. "Have you met a lot?"

"Some," she admitted. "Most of them are preeners."

"I'm too old to preen."

"No, there's more to it than that. You don't seem to have the stomach for it."

"I'm a dinosaur, kiddo," Traveler said. "I refuse to forget. I can't buy the flag waving and the noble credos. Fighting sucks, no matter what cause you carry in your back pocket. Bottom line, every sonofabitch out there with a gun in his hand feels that his god is on *his* side. It's all senseless."

Michelle's cheeks began to redden. "But you have to believe in America."

"Oh, I do," Traveler acknowledged. "But soldiering is a funny business. You meet all kinds in the field. There's no one type of soldier. Back before the war, when we were being tossed from Lebanon to El Hiagura to Nicaragua, some of us figured out that, while it may be the guys in uniform that fight the wars, it's the guys behind the desks who start them.

"The strangest thing. Sometimes when you were out killing the enemy and they were hell-bent to kill you, you'd meet up. One on one. Eye to eye. There was this *exchange* between the two of you. Not verbal. I wouldn't even call it spiritual. It was just a knowledge you shared. You realized that both of you were idiots. That both of you had guys behind desks calling the shots. That the whole theater of war around you was nothing more than a game board, that you were nothing more than a couple of toys being positioned by guys in suits whose idea of personal violence was a hangnail causing their toes to bleed underneath their three-hundred-dollar shoes."

"Then what?"

"Huh?"

"After you shared that moment . . ."

"Then we tried to blow each other's brains out."

He reached under the seat and pulled out a bottle of tequila. Unscrewing the cap with his right hand, he raised the bottle to his lips.

"You sure drink a lot," Michelle commented.

"Don't worry about it," Traveler advised. "Someday we'll be civilized enough to get cable TV back and then I can watch *Gone With The Wind* every sixteen minutes. Until that day, however . . . hello."

"What is it?"

"Is it a national holiday today?"

"Nope."

"Then this can't be a parade. Mrs. Paxton, I think you're going to get your first taste of trouble right about now."

Traveler eased the car slowly into the town. A crowd of a hundred or more people milled about in the street. Traveler pulled the car slowly over to the curb.

"What are you doing?" Michelle asked.

"We're tourists, right?"

He got out of the car and walked over to the edge of

the crowd. Michelle, cursing under her breath, followed. The town was normal enough. Pleasant one- and two-story homes. A small main street. Norman Rockwell squared. It would have been picture-postcard perfect were it not for the fires of hate in the eyes of its citizenry.

"What's going on?" Traveler asked a portly man.

"Shhh. We're having a trial."

"What kind of trial?"

"Shut up and listen."

Traveler stood on his toes to get a glimpse of what the crowd's attention was focused upon. In the middle of the town square was a large platform. A man at a podium was yelling. A young, fresh-faced boy with large brown eyes was shackled next to him.

"All right," the man yelled. "Guilty or not guilty?"

"Guilty!" the crowd screamed in unison.

"Hang him or not?"

"Hang him!" the crowd replied.

"So be it. Tomorrow, scumball, you will be hung until dead at precisely eight o'clock in the morning."

The young man with the doe eyes was shunted off the platform by two burly policemen. The man at the podium faced the crowd. "Eight o'clock, folks. After the hanging the Rosary Society will be serving breakfast in the church hall."

The crowd began to dissipate.

Traveler buttonholed the portly man at his side. "What kind of trial was that?"

"What's it to you?" the man replied, cautiously.

"Nothing. I mean, it was a great trial. But what was that boy accused of?"

"We found him packing a lot of guns in his pickup truck. We figured he was into child-napping."

"Huh?"

"Big business these days. Mercenaries come up from Mexico, round up a bunch of American kids, and take them back down south as a source of cheap labor."

"Oh," Traveler nodded. "So the boy confessed, I guess."

"Naah." The portly man smirked. "He denied everything. That's how we knew he was guilty."

"Come again?"

"Well, since the Dos Passos-Harper Act it's illegal to carry arms if you're not a lawman, official-like. So when this guy showed up we just knew he was a bandit."

"Gotcha."

Traveler glanced at Michelle. She met his gaze, deadpan. The portly man scrutinized Traveler and Michelle. His nose hairs were as long as most people's eyelashes. "You two new to these parts?"

"Yes," Traveler said, pumping the man's hand good-naturedly. "The little woman and I are heading to California. Our first vacation since the war. Been driving all day. Frankly, I'm bushed. You wouldn't have a hotel in town, would you?"

A jack-o'-lantern grin appeared on the fat man's face. "We sure do. We reopened the Holiday Inn. It's an A-one kind of place. Magic fingers in the bed. Heated pool. We even managed to restore all those black velvet tiger paintings."

"Sounds like my kind of place."

Michelle nudged Traveler. "But we were planning on driving through the night, *honey.*"

Traveler nudged her back. Hard. "But I'm plumb tuckered out, *dearest.* A good night's sleep and a good meal would really appeal to me right now."

"Then you can get up and watch the hanging tomorrow." The fat man beamed. "It should be a good one. We think this guy is connected with a large Mexican Communist conspiracy."

"You don't say," Traveler said.

"Just hearsay, but I figure it's true enough."

"Probably." Traveler nodded. "Which way is that Holiday Inn?"

The man raised a stubby paw. "Just down the block and hang a right. You can't miss it. It's the place with the balloons in front of it. You know, we even have cable TV in the rooms now. We show old movies at night. This week I think we got a saga. *Gone With The Wind.*"

Traveler grinned at Michelle. "Honey, it's one of my favorites."

He turned to the fat man. "Thank you."

"Anytime."

Traveler escorted Michelle back to the car. "What the hell are you doing?" Michelle snapped. "We're on a mission!"

"Yeah, well," Traveler said, "call me stupid, call me unpatriotic, but I have this allergic reaction to lynchings."

He pushed Michelle into the car. A look of horror spread across her face. "You're not going to do anything, are you?"

"Naaah," Traveler said, sitting behind the wheel. "I'm just a tourist, remember?"

He kicked the car into drive and cruised down the block. Michelle glared at him. "You're twisted, you know that?"

Traveler smiled to himself. "I had heard rumors . . . but it's all hearsay."

He turned the car off the main street and headed for the Holiday Inn. Even now he could feel the adrenaline pumping.

6

The jail wasn't much to speak of, a standard small-town affair that doubled as the police station. Several black-and-whites were parked outside, illuminated only by a lone streetlamp and a full moon.

Traveler ran to the back of the jail, the timing device in his hand. He had placed a wad of plastique in the gas tank of each one of the black-and-whites. The cars weren't near any populated areas. He wanted to cause havoc, not physical injuries. More than likely, a few windows would be rattled, even shattered. He figured that windows could be repaired. A broken neck, however, was hard to fix.

He took the rest of the plastique and carefully wadded it around the back window leading into the jail cells. When he was done he peeked into the prison. The young man was slouched on a bunk.

"Hey, kid," he whispered.

The boy turned his head toward the window. "Whaddaya want?"

"Better get yourself way over in the far corner."

"What for?"

"So you don't get blown into smithereens when I take out this window."

The kid showed the first real sign of interest. "You want to run that by me again, old man?"

Traveler frowned at the boy. "You're making this real easy, you know that? Look, punk, get yourself in that corner, shut your eyes and your mouth, and get ready to run like hell."

The kid gulped and did as he was told. Traveler ran behind a nearby tree and clutched the remote timer in his hand. "Okay," he whispered. "Time for fireworks."

He slowly turned the dial. In front of the prison, the three black-and-white units exploded. The noise was deafening. One car. Then the next. Then the next. Fireballs roared twenty feet into the air. Traveler heard the cries of surprise from inside the prison. The guards would, no doubt, be tumbling out of the jail right about now. He flicked the switch full to the left.

He watched the plastique around the jail-cell window flame to life. He ducked as chunks of metal and concrete thudded all around him. Tossing the remote down, he ran through the smoke and plunged a hand down through the ruptured wall. "Come on, punk, grab on."

A quivering hand emerged from the debris and clung on to Traveler's hesitantly. He yanked the boy out of the jail cell. The boy's eyes were still widened in amazement.

"Get the lead out," Traveler said. "Head for open country. They won't be able to catch you for a while. Their cars just broke down."

"Jesus," the kid gasped. "I don't get it."

"What's to get? Start running."

The kid stood there for a moment. "Why do this for me? You don't even know me."

"That's probably why I did it."

"But you don't even know whether I'm guilty or not."

"That doesn't matter. What they were going to do was wrong. But, kid?"

"Yeah?"

"One thing. If you are guilty of what they say, don't ever try it again. Because if I find out about it, if I ever even think that you're harming one kid, I'll track you down. I'll find you. I'll put a bullet through your head. Got that?"

The kid offered him a lopsided grin. "Tough guy, huh?"

"Nope," Traveler said. "Just a man who keeps his promises. Now, beat it."

Traveler watched as the kid turned and ran off into the night. A hand grasped him on his shoulder. He grabbed the hand and was about to toss his attacker headfirst into the tree when he heard a woman gasp. He whirled. It was Michelle.

"Jesus," she gasped. "Are you crazy?"

He relaxed his grip. "Sorry. Don't ever come up on me from behind again. It's not healthy."

She gaped at the plumes of smoke emanating from the front and the rear of the prison. "Why do I get the feeling we're out of plastique now?"

Traveler shrugged. "We weren't going to use it anyhow. What the hell are you doing out of the hotel?"

"I thought it might seem a little less suspicious if Mr. and Mrs. Paxton were strolling when the jail went into low orbit."

He smiled at her. "There's hope for you yet."

They linked arms and walked off down a side street, coming up on the burning squad cars a moment later. A small crowd had gathered in the street. People were tumbling out of their homes. The fat man from the lynch mob nearly knocked Traveler off his feet.

"What happened?" Traveler asked.

"The goddamned prisoner escaped," the man whined. "I knew it. I knew he was part of a Communist conspiracy. They probably have operatives all over the country by now."

Traveler nodded. He suddenly felt very weak. Very dizzy. A bolt of pain sliced through his forehead. His knees began to buckle. Michelle supported his weight. "Are you okay?"

"Sure," he said, straightening up. "Just a headache. It'll pass."

The fat man looked at him sympathetically. "I know how those are," he said. "I get 'em right over my eyes. They go clear down to my neck. Overwork. Too much pressure."

Traveler nodded numbly. The fat man turned to an elderly woman. "Hey, Mae. How about opening the drugstore for a couple of friends of mine?"

The old woman, her face illuminated by the flames, glanced at Traveler and Michelle. "What's the problem?"

"Looks like this fella could use some aspirin."

The woman scrutinized Traveler's sweating face. "Yeah. You do look a little feverish. You got cash?"

Traveler nodded. "Yeah."

"Okay. Come on, then."

The woman walked off toward a small drugstore off the town square. Traveler turned to the fat man. "Thanks. Thanks a lot."

"No problem. My father used to say, 'Money doesn't mean anything. It's your health. As long as you have your health, you have everything.' "

Traveler smiled. Michelle gripped his arm tighter. They followed the old woman toward the drugstore.

"You just had to get involved, didn't you?" she said under her breath.

"I always get involved," he muttered. "That's the problem."

"You're not the killing machine you make yourself out to be," she said in a mocking tone.

"Oh, I'm that all right," Traveler said. "It's just that I have these little flaws. Being human is one of them."

"How's your head?"

"Hurts like hell."

They walked in silence a half block behind the shuffling old woman.

"You meant what you said to that boy, didn't you? About killing him? I heard all that."

"Yeah."

"You're weird."

"What's not?" Traveler said. "I mean, here you have a town willing to lynch a man without a fair trial. The same people who cheered his hanging, planned a breakfast around it, will take pity on a total stranger with a bad headache. Tell me that doesn't strike you as laughable."

"Not laughable," Michelle replied. "Sad, somehow."

"Yeah," Traveler sighed. "Sad and human."

They stepped into the drugstore as the old woman turned on the lights. "I have some extra-strength headache tablets," the old woman said. "Two bucks a bottle."

Traveler fished in his pocket and pulled out a ten-dollar bill. "Give me five bottles."

The old woman shot him an inquisitive look. "You planning to make a hobby out of getting headaches?"

Traveler offered her a smile with the money. "I get tense when I'm away from home. You never know what you'll run up against."

"I hear you," the old woman said, returning his smile. "You poor folks ride into our town thinking it's a real peaceful place and wind up seeing a Fourth of July show."

"Something like that," Traveler said, scooping up the bottles. He stuck them in the pockets of his ill-fitting sport coat. "Thanks for opening up."

"No trouble."

Traveler and Michelle walked out of the drugstore. Fire trucks were screaming toward the jailhouse now. Their sirens caused Traveler's ears to explode. Michelle grabbed on to his right arm. "Are you sure you're okay?"

"Yeah," Traveler said, massaging his forehead with his free hand. "I'm getting too old for this crap."

"Now what?" the woman asked.

"Well, we can go back to the hotel and try out those magic fingers in bed."

"Sure," she said. "By the way, I changed rooms. We now have two single beds. You can play with your magic fingers all night long if you like."

Traveler smirked. "And I thought this would be a second honeymoon."

"Go to hell," she shot back.

"I've been there," Traveler said, suddenly feeling very old and very obsolete. "It's not all it's cracked up to be."

7

He was in the jungle again, together with Hill, Orwell, and Margolin. They were up to their necks in trouble and they knew it. They weren't supposed to be in El Hiagura. Officially they were military advisers. But there they were, armed to the teeth, surrounded by guerrillas.

Traveler was walking point. As usual. He heard a hissing noise. It wasn't a bomb. It wasn't a shell incoming. He didn't like the sound of it.

He trotted back to the others. "Something's wrong here," he had time to say before the chirping crickets roared to life around him. Their screeches sounded like gigantic birds of prey. He tried to scream. The effort got caught in his throat. He heard the guerrillas bellowing from behind the underbrush. The whole earth began to shake.

Gunshots. His lungs were filled with the acrid smell

of gunpowder. He was choking on it. He fell to the ground, colliding with it painfully. Shards of pain exploded all over his body. He turned to look at the others. They were writhing on the ground. The sun exploded in front of him, whiting out his vision. He felt the sweat drops launch themselves from his tingling skin.

He thrashed this way and that.

In the distance his father stood, holding a carton of milk. Bullet holes ripped through the carton. The white gushes of the milk soon turned to crimson and his father fell to the floor of the jungle, choking on his own blood.

His wife and child ran up to the old man and stood there for one horrible second before exploding into flames with a sickening screech.

Traveler opened his eyes suddenly. The ceiling of the hotel room spun around him.

He grasped the night table at his side, fumbling in the darkness. He smelled his own sweat. The room lit up momentarily before fading into blackness again.

"Are you looking for these?" Michelle asked, holding out a bottle of the aspirin.

Traveler sat up in his bed. "Yeah, thanks." He took the bottle and poured six aspirin down his parched throat.

Michelle, fully clothed, sat on the edge of the bed next to him. "Bad one, huh?"

Traveler nodded. "Yeah. Every once in a while I party with ghosts when the lights go out."

The woman nodded. "It's almost six. You feel up to going on?"

Traveler slowly got out of the bed. "Yeah. The night air will do me good."

The two packed their belongings in silence. It was the worst nightmare Traveler had experienced in over a year. He was dying, he knew, so maybe it was some sort of reconciliation. Maybe his beleaguered brain was trying to conjure up the past, the wisps of the horror Traveler had experienced, and exorcise it all. Maybe. Or maybe his brain was collapsing from within. Maybe the cancer would spread and Traveler would die a babbling, out-of-control lunatic.

He walked in silence to the car and slid in behind the wheel. The woman tossed her bags in the backseat and shot Traveler a concerned look. "You okay to drive?"

"Fine," Traveler said, cracking the engine to life. "Just fine. If I highball it, we can make the boat by dusk."

Traveler stood on the gas for the entire drive. By nightfall they reached Long Beach. Traveler paid a pimply-faced attendant three dollars and guided the Subaru into the crowded parking lot. Illuminated by the moonlight and the garish, carnival-like lamps strung from high poles, the dock looked positively eerie. It resembled a faded postcard from an amusement park gone to seed.

"You can still back out of this, you know," Traveler said to Michelle.

"I appreciate your concern," she said, climbing out of the car, "but I already have a father."

Traveler grit his teeth and stepped out of the car. Michelle went to the trunk. "Leave the weapons there," Traveler said. "For all we know, they'll have metal detectors on board."

"You expect me to go out there unarmed?" Michelle said. "I thought you were kidding."

"Nope," Traveler said. He pulled his combat knife from around his belt and buried it in a suitcase filled with camera equipment. "If we're going to do this, we're going to have to do it right. Enter packing guns and we'll exit really quickly."

"I don't like this," the woman said.

"I'm not crazy about it myself."

Carrying three suitcases between them they walked out to the yacht that would take them to Arrowhead Island. Boarding the gaily-colored vessel, they were glad-handed by a swarthy man with enough scars on his face to qualify him for the Rand McNally map hall of fame.

"Welcome aboard," he said in an Eastern European accent. He addressed both of them, but his eyes remained solely on Michelle, his gaze sliding up and down her legs like 20/20 pistons. Traveler glanced around. The yacht was tacky. Piped Hawaiian music belched from small speakers scattered around the deck. The crew wore plastic leis.

"You are fortunate," the captain said. "This is our last trip out to the Island tonight."

"Great," Traveler said. "We've always been the lucky type."

The captain continued to ogle Michelle. "If there's anything I can help you with, any questions I can answer . . ."

"There is one thing," Traveler said, smiling. The captain was forced to look in his direction.

"Yes?"

"Why are you guys dressed like Don Ho when we're heading toward Mexico?"

The captain sputtered. Michelle laughed silently. Traveler took her by the arm and led her farther down the deck. "Come, my dear."

They walked to a bar area on deck. Michelle was still smiling. "You can be a real wise-ass, you know that?"

"I had to say something. Our captain's eyes were about to launch themselves onto your thighs."

"Hmm. A gentleman too."

"I have my weak moments. Want a drink?"

"Bourbon and water."

Traveler ordered two drinks. He glanced at the captain over his shoulder. The skipper was on the phone. "I don't like this whole setup," Traveler said, smiling for effect as he sipped his drink. "Did you catch his accent? If that guy's name is Green, my name is Heidi."

The Muzak launched into an insipid rendition of "Tiny Bubbles" as the yacht headed out to sea. A sudden premonition of danger wriggled up and down Traveler's spine. He began to sweat.

The captain was cupping the receiver of the phone in his hand.

"What's up?" Michelle asked.

"For the first time I'm beginning to feel that old Orwell was right about this assignment. It's going to be hairy, all right."

"Is that logic or instinct talking?"

"Both. I have a feeling that scarface over there is the one who checks out the possible marks for the snatch. Right now, I'd guess we just passed muster as possible targets."

"How can you tell?"

"The guy is talking into the phone like he's trying out for a remake of *Casablanca.* I think it was your legs that did it."

"What's wrong with my legs?"

Traveler glanced at her legs. For the first time he noticed that they were strong, shapely, young. He grinned, in spite of the feeling of danger. "Nothing. They're great."

The female agent found herself blushing. "Well, I usually run every day."

"That'll come in handy," Traveler said, returning his attention to the captain. "I think we may wind up doing quite a bit of running on this trip."

8

The sounds of laughter filled the room. Traveler sat on the end of his bed. He heard Michelle humming to herself in the shower. It was almost midnight, but still, on Arrowhead Island, the partying continued. He lit a cigarette and took a drag, exhaling slowly.

Two small portholes allowed him a view of the ocean. He hated confinement. After the war his nervous system was so shattered that he couldn't be around even small crowds of people without having an involuntary seizure. Maybe that's why he had loved the Southwest so much. Big sky. Big country. He shivered involuntarily. The room seemed to be closing in on him.

He stood, put out the cigarette, and had a quick shot of tequila. He walked to the bureau, pulled out a tie and a clean shirt, and with halfhearted enthusiasm, went about the task of making himself look presentable.

An orchestra downstairs somewhere was playing an overbloated rendition of "New York, New York." People were beginning to stagger into their suites now. He could hear laughter and slurred speech from the hallway outside.

He grimaced in the mirror, knowing that this, probably his last battle, would be started in what amounted to a floating pleasure palace. There was some irony to that. Perhaps it was just as well he was going to die soon. He had lived most of his life in a world where violence and mayhem were givens. Maybe he just wouldn't fit in with this new wave of trendiness.

A bolt of pain slammed into his forehead. He popped two more aspirin as Michelle walked into the room. He blinked twice in amazement.

"What's the matter?" she asked.

"N-nothing," he said, his throat getting dry. It had been a very long time since he had seen a woman dressed for a night on the town. Over two decades. He simply wasn't used to the sight. She wore a blue outfit, skirt, blouse, small scarf, which served to accent the blondness of her hair. In the dim light of the cabin, she was positively angelic.

"Let me fix that," she said, walking forward to fiddle with the double Windsor knot on his tie.

"Men can never get this right," she muttered.

Traveler actually blushed. "Well, I haven't done this . . . the last time was . . . my son's third birthday."

"There. You're looking pretty good for a mercenary." She smiled.

"You're looking mighty fine for an agent."

"Well," she said. "Shall we mingle?"

"If we have to."

"We have to."

She took him by the arm and they left the cabin. The two walked down the corridor to the elevator leading to the play tier. As they descended the noise from the crowd and the belching of the different bands rose up to meet them. Cigarette smoke hung heavily in the air. By the time they reached the casino pits, their vision was partially obscured.

Traveler led the woman through the crowds. Small areas were partitioned off into different sections: gambling, dining, cabaret, bar.

"I'm not much for gambling," Traveler said.

"I've never tried it," Michelle replied. "Maybe we should start with a drink. We can work our way up to slot machines if we get really daring."

Traveler nodded. He knew that they were here for a purpose but, surrounded by the noise, the laughter, the music, and having Michelle on his arm, he suddenly felt almost buoyant. He may have been playing at having a good time but right now he was doing a damn good job of acting.

The two of them walked into the bar section and took a seat. A waitress who apparently had never mastered the art of blouse buttoning leaned over Traveler. "What'll you have?" she said.

"Double shot of tequila," he said, gazing at her breasts straining against the flimsy blouse.

"What about the lady?" the waitress asked him.

"She has a voice." Traveler smiled into her nipples. "You can ask her yourself."

The waitress shrugged and turned to Michelle. The agent smiled icily. "Bourbon and water."

The waitress nodded and walked over to the bar. "Nice outfit," Traveler said.

"I hadn't noticed," the woman replied. "Now. What's the plan?"

Traveler slouched in his chair. "I don't know. Eat. Drink. Be merry. And talk to any and all strangers that chat us up . . . within limits, of course."

"Meaning?"

"Meaning I don't want you to do anything stupid, like walking out with any asshole because you think he may be our guy. You could just as easily get rolled or worse by some of the sea scum on this barge."

"Don't be paranoid."

"Paranoid? End of the bar. Next to the closed-circuit TV."

Michelle glanced at the bar. Nestled under a closed-circuit television, showing the action from the casino section, were three of the nastiest-looking individuals she had ever seen. They were big. Burly. Pockmarked.

"You have good eyes for . . ." Michelle said.

"Someone my age?" Traveler smirked.

"For an untrained operative." She smiled sweetly.

The waitress somehow managed to prevent her breasts from bursting forth as she delivered the drinks. Traveler watched her sway away. "I could get to like this place," he mused, raising a glass to Michelle.

She smirked, returning his toast. "To the future."

"The future," Traveler said merrily. What the hell. He didn't have one, so he might as well drink to hers.

"Let's dance," Michelle said suddenly.

"Hey, I'm not—"

"Oh, come on. Just one, all right?"

Traveler rolled his eyes and allowed himself to be dragged out onto the dance floor. An alleged song was being played by an eight-piece group who had apparently learned the finer elements of rhythm from watching old Johnny Weissmuller movies.

Traveler attempted to get his body to move to the beat. Michelle laughed, slipping easily into the crush of bodies around them. Traveler found himself amazingly stiff-jointed on the dance floor. It didn't help that he was wearing a suit. His tie bothered him. His shoes pinched his feet. Worse yet, he felt old. He was sure he resembled the Tin Woodsman from *The Wizard of Oz* executing a bad frug. The woman agent didn't seem to mind. "You're not half bad," she said.

"I'm all bad," Traveler wheezed.

He was forced to laugh at his own awkwardness. He felt vulnerable on the dance floor, but pleasantly so. He hadn't experienced such a relaxed sensation since Roberta was alive. You had to trust somebody to let down your guard. He was letting himself go now, in front of Michelle Trinen. Granted, it was part of his job, but still . . . it felt good.

The dance sputtered to a halt.

"Ten minootz," the band leader announced. "Break thime."

Traveler and Michelle linked arms as they walked back to their table. He stiffend somewhat. His head began to tingle.

"What's up?" she asked.

"Trouble," he muttered.

Then he saw them, two smiling young men, dressed to the nines, walking alongside them.

"You looked pretty good out there, dad," one of the men said to Traveler. Traveler clenched his free hand. "Thanks, son. I try to keep in shape."

The first man felt Traveler's bicep and whistled through his teeth. "Solid."

"Yeah," the other said. "You and your daughter can dance up a storm. You stole the spotlight."

"Wife," Traveler corrected.

"Oh, hey, sorry," the first one apologized melodramatically.

"Don't worry about it," Michelle said with a smile. "I'm sure you two can find children your own age here to dance with."

Clutching Traveler's arm, she guided him back to the table. He was smiling. He liked the way she handled herself.

They sat down next to each other. Michelle pulled her chair closer. "I'm glad you didn't overreact," she said.

"Me?" Traveler replied. "Naaah."

"Good. Because I'm sure I've seen one of their faces before. On a computer printout. I can't remember the name but he was involved in gunrunning. Mexico. A year back. They may be the talent scouts."

"Maybe," Traveler said, glancing at the far end of the bar. The three Cro-Magnon Coors guzzlers were gone.

"I'll be right back," Michelle said.

"Where you going?"

"To powder my nose, *dear,*" she said, rising. "I'll be back in a minute."

"If you're not back in two, I'm coming after you."

"I can take care of myself."

He watched her fade into the crowd. Traveler sat, nursing a drink. The word *if* kept on running through his mind. *If* he were ten years younger. *If* she were ten years older. *If* the world was different. *If* . . .

"Hey, ain't I seen you around before?" asked an older voice.

Traveler glanced at the elderly man in the security guard's outfit standing next to his table.

"Maybe," Traveler said, extending a hand. "Kiel Paxton's the name. I sell hardware. Vegas."

The old man pumped his hand. "Naaah. I know you from somewhere else. Ever pass through New Mexico?"

Traveler smiled, gritting his teeth. Great. All he had to do now was run into someone who recognized him as a merc. "Nope. Never."

"Well, you put me in mind of a fella I met a few years back. Maybe ten years now. A soldier of fortune."

"You don't say."

"Oh, yeah. Yeah. He was something. Killed over a hundred roadrats. Saved our camp. Then he just took off. Never got a chance to thank him."

"Well"—Traveler nodded—"I'm sure he knew you were grateful."

The old man nodded. "I'd keep an eye on your wife if I were you."

"Huh?"

"She's young. She's pretty."

"I'm lucky to have her."

"That you are, but that's not what I was talking about. We've had some robberies on board lately.

And"—he leaned in closer—"other things I'm not supposed to talk about."

"Uh-huh."

"I just wouldn't want to see anything happen to either one of you. You seem like a really nice couple. You deserve to be happy."

"Thanks," Traveler said, not really understanding where the conversation was leading. "Uh, why do you say that?"

"Oh, I get the idea that you've been knocked around a lot."

"No more than most."

"Well," the old man said, "that's what life is all about, right? Getting knocked down and having the gumption to get back up again."

"It sure is."

The old man leaned over Traveler before leaving the table. "All the happiness in the world to you, sir. By the way, Mr. Hardware Salesman from Las Vegas, you might want to pull down your right sleeve. Those pointy-star things that you toss at roadrats are showing from under your cuff."

Traveler glanced down at his right hand. He cursed his stupidity. He had left on his wristband, housing his deadly ninja shuriken, weapons he hurled during intense bouts of one-on-one combat. He looked up at the old man, helplessly.

The old man winked. "Don't worry about a thing. We all deserve to let the past be the past. Enjoy your future, stranger. You helped a lot of us enjoy ours."

The security guard backed away. "Now, if I were you, I'd go looking for that wife of yours. Have a good one."

The guard continued on his rounds. Traveler smiled to himself. He glanced over his shoulder. Michelle was rounding the bar, heading toward the table. The security guard had made him feel good. Maybe there had been a purpose to his surviving the Nuke-Out after all. Maybe he had brought some good to the world. Maybe his life as a hired killer had actually tipped the scales of justice in a more positive direction than he had ever acknowledged.

He quietly slipped the wristband and the shurikens off his wrist, placing them in his vest pocket.

He glanced over his shoulder, prepared to meet Michelle's smile with an even wider one of his own.

He gaped at the dance floor before him.

There was no smile awaiting him.

Michelle was gone.

9

Traveler fought the fear welling up in his chest as he bolted from the bar section into the crowded casino looking for any sign of the woman. The laughter that moments before had seemed light and gleeful now struck him as being nothing more than grotesque braying. The smiling faces around him now appeared to be twisted into hard, leering gargoyle faces.

The cigarette smoke filled his lungs with a rank, gritty sensation. Garish, half-besotted slobs hung over the slot machines. Women in pancake makeup clotted by sweat leaned onto the roulette wheels. Half-naked women with dark circles under their eyes gyrated on a stage to a droning disco beat.

The lights irritated his eyes. The din reverberated through his ears. He could hear his heart pounding faster and faster as the panic grew.

They had gotten her. He knew that. But for what

purpose? He hoped against hope that she had just gone out for some fresh air. Maybe met a friend.

He cursed himself for allowing her to come along. He should have done this solo. Damn Orwell. Damn Michelle for being so willing a victim.

He plunged through the nearly deserted dining area and took the escalator up to the top deck. It was almost empty. The swimming pool, the shuffleboard decks were deserted. Only a few people congregated at a small bar at the end of the deck.

Traveler marched down to the bar. The bartender, a short, redheaded woman, dried a glass, a cigarette dangling from her cracked lips.

"Have you seen a woman?" Traveler asked.

"Lots of them." She shrugged. "Wanna drink?"

"A shot of tequila," Traveler said, trying to regain his composure. He shouldn't care about people. The more you care, the more you're hurt. It was a lesson he had yet to learn.

The bartender handed him his shot. He downed it immediately. "Who're you looking for?" the bartender asked. "Girlfriend? Party girl?"

"My wife."

The woman nodded. "Don't worry about it. They always show up. Sometimes they get on this barge, see a younger guy—"

"She's not like that," Traveler snapped.

"None of 'em are," the bartender replied.

Traveler couldn't believe it. He was jealous. Protective of Michelle's good reputation. What the hell was going on here? They were on a mission together. He didn't even *know* the woman. He took a deep breath.

She wasn't his wife. She wasn't his lover. She was just a government flunky working for an agency he despised.

"Don't worry, old man," the bartender said. "She'll be back."

Traveler sighed under the words. He was forty-six now. Feeling his age. Feeling more like a dinosaur with every passing moment. He had never thought about his age before. He was a topflight warrior. That's how he made his living. But now, with death looming in the near future, with his heart suddenly activated by the presence of a warm, intelligent woman, he felt ancient.

He leaned over the bar.

"You love her?" came a female voice.

Traveler turned and saw a young girl standing next to him. She was young, shapely. Her hair was long and dark. Her almond-colored skin sparkled in the moonlight.

Traveler nodded.

The woman flashed a dazzling set of teeth. "This is a second honeymoon for you two?"

Traveler tensed. She was to be his bait. He was sure of it. He resisted the impulse to stick his left foot down her throat and jog around the top deck. She was in league with whoever had Michelle.

He flashed a sheepish grin. "Our first. We've only been married three years. My job . . . the way times were . . . we just never got the chance to get away."

The young woman nodded her head. She suddenly crossed her arms in front of her chest, pushing her breasts up and nearly out of her saronglike gown. "It's getting cold out here."

"A little."

"Maybe your wife met a younger man and decided to have a fling," the woman said bluntly.

Traveler stared at her.

The woman continued to hug herself. Her left nipple began to peek out from behind the top of the dress. "She is younger than you?"

"Uh-huh. About ten years."

The young woman shrugged. "Some young women are foolish like that. They are attracted to young peacocks. Myself? I am attracted to older men."

She took the slice of lemon from the side of Traveler's shot glass and placed it to her lips. Slowly, deliberately, she ran her tongue along it before taking a juicy bite out of its core, exposing her teeth all the while.

Traveler watched a teardrop of lemon juice dribble from her lips, over her chin, and down her long, swanlike neck. The drop of juice disappeared between her breasts.

"Well," Traveler said, "actually, I'm not *that* old."

The woman laughed softly. "Prove it," she whispered.

Traveler cleared his throat. "Umm, I really should go downstairs and look for my wife."

The woman took him by the arm. "I will take the escalator down with you. Maybe you will walk me to my door?"

"Sure."

Traveler allowed himself to be led toward the escalator. The presence of this woman on his arm irritated him. Funny, only moments before he had relished the weight of Michelle's arm there. He tried to get a fix on the woman's accent. It was foreign, to be sure, but from an area he couldn't identify. She had a strange, singsongish delivery that was half coquettish, half pigeon. She could be Hawaiian, he supposed.

She stood on the step below him on the escalator, leaning ever so gently against his chest. He glanced down at her. She had pulled the top of her dress down slightly, allowing him the chance to see both of her nipples.

By the time they reached the living quarters area, she had readjusted it. They stepped off the escalator into a dimly lit hallway.

"I am down here. At the very end."

He nodded, following her down the hall. He placed the key in her door. He heard the latch click. Instinctively he tensed his body. If the young woman noticed, she betrayed no signs of the fact.

"Would you like to come in for a nightcap?" she asked.

"Well, maybe just one."

He entered the room. She didn't turn on the light. Immediately he sensed the presence of others in the room. In a blinding flash the pupils of his eyes suddenly dilated, acclimating themselves to the darkness.

The swiftness of his biological reaction caught him by surprise. The room seemed suddenly well lit, although he realized he was still totally in the dark.

He saw the three thugs from the bar and one of the pretty boys from the dance floor.

The gigolo approached him from behind. Without uttering a word, Traveler pivoted his body and sent his left elbow crashing into the boy's windpipe. He heard the man gasp and stagger backward, falling over a table.

"What the fuck is going on?" he heard the girl hiss. Her voice didn't seem as melodic as before. Vaguely reptilian.

The three burly men rushed forward. One of them had a gun. Traveler tensed. His first instinct was to defend himself. He knew he could take out at least two of the remaining three men. He checked himself, though. That was the act of a mercenary, not of a hardware salesman from Vegas.

He heard the hiss of a pellet.

Trank gun, he theorized.

Before his mind could stop his body, he began to leap out of the way. Catching himself halfway through the move, he halted and turned.

The dart smacked into his forehead, exploding into his already tortured brain.

Traveler let out a scream as he fell onto the ground.

"Oh, jeez," he heard a voice say as darkness rose up to greet him.

He felt his body tumble through furniture. He grasped the air around him feebly. Soon he was on the floor. Flashes of light blinded him. His brain whirled. His arms and legs flailed about.

"Damn. He moved!" another voice thundered.

"What's going on?" the girl demanded.

"Don't turn on that light!" someone else commanded.

"Is he dead?" asked a male voice.

The boy continued to wheeze.

"Tend to Johnny."

"I'm spitting up blood, man. He almost broke my neck. Jesus! Look at his head! Did you kill him?"

"No. No. He's still moving."

"Now what do we do?"

"We have to take him."

"I don't know about this."

"Look, he was the one we picked. We already got his old lady. What do we do? Throw them both overboard? We'll wind up at the bottom of that swamp if word ever gets out about this."

"Shut up! I have to think."

"What the hell is going on?" the girl whined.

"Clean up his head. He's out."

"But is he dead?"

"Did you ever see a dead man breathe before?"

"Our ass is gonna be grass if *he* ever finds out about this."

"Who's gonna tell him? Are you gonna tell him?"

"No, I'm not going to tell him."

"Okay. Okay. Get a washcloth. Hurry it up."

"What's going on?" the girl asked again.

"Shut up, bitch. Turn on the light."

A light switch clicked on somewhere nearby. It didn't expell the darkness. The voices became lower, muffled. The bolts of different-colored lightning gradually subsided. He was floating now, floating on air. No, someone was lifting him. That was it. Someone was lifting him.

Taking him to his last mission.

10

Voices swirled around him as he hovered in and out of unconsciousness. He wasn't on the ship anymore. Of that he was certain. The air was thick, hot and humid. He could hear the sounds of birds crying out in the distance. He tried to shake his mind clear, but his mind would have none of it.

His head seemed to explode in a succession of never-ending discharges. Pinpricks of pain tingled incessantly. His body seemed alternately heavy and light. Every time he tried to open his eyes, to shout, to move, he felt another needle plunged into his arm.

The voices, all male, hovered outside his ear, making constant verbal sounds resembling a hummingbird. At times he could make out the words. Most of the time, however, the voices were nothing more than a constant hum.

"I can't believe your stupidity."

"It wasn't our fault. He moved."

"Sedate him. I want to check for damage."

He was strapped onto something now. A gurney of some sort. He could tell by the swaying of his body that he was being wheeled somewhere. Heels on tile. A corridor. Squeaking hinge. Swinging door. He was lifted gently onto something else. Something that slid forward.

"Back away. Back away."

"But it looks like he's coming to!"

"If he does, it will only be momentarily. He has enough drugs in him to open a pharmacy."

A whirring sound. Above him. To his left. To his right. He opened his eyes a crack. He was in a chamber of some sort. The chamber was whirling about him. He felt like an astronaut. Maybe that was it. Maybe he was in deep space. He had made it at last. He felt his consciousness ebb. The chamber retreated into the back of his mind.

His head sagged to the left.

"This can't be right."

"Why not?"

"Because it can't, that's why. Prep him again."

Wheels. Doors. Whirring. Voices. Far off. Echoing. "I apologize to you boys. You might have sent us the ideal specimen."

"Gee, thanks."

"Don't get a big head over it. I realize that you had no idea of knowing. Let me see his things."

The whirring faded away.

When he awoke he found himself sitting in a hospital bed, strapped securely down. He adjusted his eyes to the light, squinting so as to filter out its incredible brightness. His head was throbbing. It sounded like a marching beat. He shut his eyes, realizing that he was listening to his own heart.

He blinked several times, slowly allowing the images around him to register in his brain. The room was small, well kept, and bright. He turned his head slowly to his left. Outside the window was thick, green foliage. Jungle foliage. On the other side of the wall, clipped to metal bars, was a series of X rays. More than X rays, really. Profiles of the head splashed with vivid colors.

He was curious. But more than that, he was exhausted.

The door opened slightly. Two of the three Cro-Magnons from Arrowhead walked in sullenly. They were followed by a short, thin man in his mid-thirties. He wore a white smock. His face was smooth and boyish. His eyes were an almost transparent gray. "Ah," the tiny man said, a bounce in his step, "you're awake. Good. Good."

Traveler tried to speak. His mouth was too dry. One of the Cro-Magnons held out a tube of water, the kind used by long-distance runners. They stuck the curved straw in his mouth and squeezed the plastic bottle. He sucked down the water eagerly.

"Welcome to my little world, Mr. Paxton," the doctor said, pulling up a chair.

"My name is Stanley." He smiled. "No need to reply. I already know your name as well as your wife's."

Traveler managed to squeeze out a few words. "Is she . . . ?"

"She's fine. She's just indisposed at the moment."

He pointed to the X rays on the wall across from

him. "See those? You might say that those portraits represent what make you tick. I am honored to have you here."

Traveler glared at the man. "I didn't seem to have too much of a choice about accepting your invitation."

"True. True. But I'm sure you'll find your stay here challenging nonetheless."

Traveler stared at him in silence. The little man laughed casually. "Oh, I know you want an explanation. And you shall have it. Would you like to rest now or are you up for the entire spiel? It's quite fascinating."

Traveler nodded. "I've rested enough."

"Well, my name is James Stanley. I'm a scientist, mostly taught by my father. A man whose name you may not know but, as I will explain later, you are quite familiar with. My father dabbled in genetics, biology, chemistry. He was, in actual fact, a genius. He worked for various governments before the war, and after the disaster subsided, dedicated himself to teaching me everything he could. He was slowly dying of radiation poisoning, you see. He had about ten years left and he wanted me to carry on in the family tradition.

"Oh, the knowledge he gave me during those ten years. It was a real eye-opener. I have extended that knowledge over the years. I don't mean to sound immodest, but I believe I have surpassed my father in several fields of endeavor."

Traveler smirked. "I'd applaud but my hands seem to be tied."

"A mere precaution. We can dispense with that later."

The little man rested his feet on the edge of Traveler's bed. "Well, as you know, since the war various governments have been regrouping. Now, I don't see that as a positive thing. To me all politicians are essentially evil. They usually have their own private interests at heart and their goals are remarkably short-term. In my opinion this postnuclear world should be run by one or more visionaries, Renaissance men dedicated to advancing all species of life."

"Men such as yourself?" Traveler said. He had heard this routine before.

"Yes, point of fact. But how, you might ask, can a fellow such as myself, totally unschooled in the art of combat, make a dent in the societies that are currently springing up around the globe?"

"By hiring thugs like the ones in this room?"

"In part, yes. But you can do only so much with mercenaries, as I'm sure you're well aware of. No. In order to convince the world of my serious intentions, of my very real desire to totally alter the future of humanity, I was forced to study. To think. To dream. To conceive of a weapon unsurpassed in the history of warfare."

Traveler blanched.

Dr. Stanley chuckled. "Oh, no. Not a nuclear or thermonuclear device. Far too dangerous. We've ravaged the earth enough, don't you think? No, I had to come up with something a bit more personal, a bit more theatrical, a bit more impressive. It's something I call the 'hunter-seeker.' It's been working now for over a year. Developing its skills. Realizing its potential. A few months ago I decided I had to test out my work. See if, under very conventional standards, it could live up to my expectations. But in order to test it, I had to have humans to challenge it. To fight it."

"Like me?"

"No, not like you." Stanley laughed. "No one, this far, has come close to your potential. Anyhow, a few of my associates and I decided that the best place to go shopping for our test subjects was the Arrowhead Island complex. It's only five hours away by boat. There were enough people there to choose from. Enough of a crowd to get lost in. Enough boats in the area to camouflage any smuggling activities we arranged.

"I had no prerequisites. I simply told my associates to pick men who were young and strong and were in the company of a female. In truth, you are a bit older than most of my subjects, but I think that will work out for the best."

"So," Traveler theorized, "you set the men up. You played on their affection for their wives or lovers. Arranged the women's disappearances. I suppose most of the men would have been jealous. Resentful. Even willing to go on a fling of their own as a kind of marital revenge. Then, when your Lolita showed up, flashing her tits, she'd lead them willingly into her stateroom where they'd run headfirst into a trank gun."

"Excellent," Stanley beamed. "Spoken like a true military man well versed in strategy."

Traveler shot him an uneasy stare.

"Oh, yes. I know your background. I realize that, now, you are in retirement, operating a hardware store and all, but I trust that your reflexes are still intact."

Traveler relaxed somewhat. His cover hadn't been blown. "Because of your agility," Stanley continued, "you upset my men's aim. The tranquilizer pellet hit you square in the forehead. When you were brought here I feared that we had lost you. That would have been a shame. Then we would have had to have disposed of both you and your wife without even entering you into our test program. I took an X ray of your skull. I was quite surprised at the results."

Traveler turned his head toward the window. "So. You know. I have brain cancer. Terminal."

Stanley let out a laugh that nearly knocked him out of his chair. "You poor man. You don't have any such thing. Why, any geneticist could have seen that."

Traveler faced the man. "I'm not dying of cancer?"

"On the contrary, Mr. Paxton," Stanley said, patting Traveler on the knee. "You are just beginning to live. To really live. I must admit the X rays puzzled me. There was something in your brain, all right, but it wasn't anything natural. It wasn't something caused by radiation, either.

"So, I decided to take a CAT scan of your brain. Computerized axial tomography scanners allow us to see the structure of the brain, Mr. Paxton. The CAT scan showed me that something was indeed changing your brain, both the left and right hemispheres. In layman's terms, something was altering both your intellectual and emotional makeup.

"I decided to try a PET scan. It's the big brother of the CAT."

"And those are the results?" Traveler said, gazing at the colorful X rays across the room.

"Uh-huh. Indeed they are. And they're quite remarkable. A PET scan tracks brain activity. We can actually photograph what's going on chemically inside the brain.

"You see, human brain metabolism varies according to the activities of the moment. We pretty much can sense when the metabolism is normal. What we do with a PET is inject a radioactively tagged substance into the body and then track it and see what parts of the brain are up to snuff and what parts are malfunctioning. We can actually *map* the brain. Your 'maps' were quite revealing.

"There's no cancer up there, Mr. Paxton, but there is an amazing chemical imbalance. It is as if some alien enzyme, some new element, has been added to your chemical makeup. When I saw the scans I deduced that something was causing your mind to race like a motor. All your neural networks are firing like crazy. Essentially, your brain is being kicked into high gear, it's 'on' all the time. Chemical and electrical signals are constantly being discharged.

"I must admit I was puzzled at first. Then I put two and two together, and what I got was my father."

Traveler blinked. "I'm not following this anymore."

"As I said"—Stanley beamed—"my father was one hell of a genius. Shortly before the war he was working for the United States government on something he felt would revolutionize conventional combat. A neurotoxin. An enzyme that would, in gaseous form, completely paralyze entire armies. Their sensory perception would be heightened to the point where it would cause total insanity.

"Of course it was very hush-hush and, by Geneva Convention standards, quite illegal. It was arranged to have the toxin tested on the sly in a small Central American country."

"El Hiagura," Traveler mumbled.

"Correct. Only four Caucasians, four Americans, were accidentally exposed to it. They were sent back to America. My father was about to examine them when the war happened. He never did see exactly what effects his invention caused. He would have loved to have met you, Lieutenant."

"All right, so I was exposed to your father's joy juice. So what?"

"So," Stanley said. "So, even after two and a half decades, the stuff is still in your system. In fact, I would guess that it's been dormant for at least five or ten years, correct?"

Traveler nodded. "I learned to control it."

"Excellent. A tribute to man's adaptability. However, during that time period, it has been at work, Mr. Paxton. Undermining the cellular activity in your brain. Changing it. Altering it forever. Sending it on a new course."

"What are you trying to tell me?"

"In effect, Mr. Paxton, you are mutating into something, cerebrally, *more* than human."

Traveler swallowed hard. "Am I supposed to be excited about this?"

"Oh, you should be," Stanley enthused. "You are evolving into the ultimate human warrior. Someone who can sense everything. Someone who will not be overwhelmed by the overstimulation caused by the neurotoxin."

"Okay," Traveler said. "So I'm going to be a human

bloodhound soon. What does that have to do with what you're doing down here?"

"Don't you see? I have created, genetically, the ultimate nonhuman hunter. You are the ultimate human. It will be my greatest test, the ultimate in Darwinistic warfare. In the jungle it's survival of the fittest. In a short time we will see exactly what species is destined to alter the course of human history."

Traveler stared at the man's glazed gray eyes. He had the feeling that, in spite of his genius tag, Stanley could use a lot more furniture in his attic. "And what if I don't want to take part in this grand test?" Traveler asked.

Stanley bounced up off the chair. "Then I will kill both you and your wife in a slow, barbaric manner."

"Just checking," Traveler said, with a smirk.

"Please, don't be upset, Mr. Paxton. Your presence here is a godsend. You will play a direct part in the shaping of the new world. Doesn't that fill you with a sense of pride?"

"Can I get back to you on that?"

"Now. Rest for a little while. Then you and your wife will have dinner with me. At the end of dinner you will get a chance to meet your opponent."

Traveler watched the man walk out of the room. "I'll save room for dessert."

One of the three burly guards walked up to Traveler's bed. "You got a smart mouth, you know that?"

Traveler flashed him a toothy grin. "I'm a smart guy. Didn't you hear the doc?"

The big man muttered something under his breath

and left the room. Traveler sighed and attempted to sleep, in spite of the straps tethering him to the bed. He figured he'd best catch up on his sleep now. After tonight he probably wouldn't be getting a lot of it.

11

Stanley sat at the head of the enormous banquet table. There was enough room at the table to seat twelve. Only three people, however, sat in the massive dining room. Traveler picked at his food. Across from him, clad in an evening gown, sat Michelle. They had allowed Stanley to hold court the entire evening, not exchanging more than a look or two.

She had a bruise under her left eye. A split lip. There were marks around her wrist where she had either been chained or tethered. Traveler figured he would find identical marks around her ankles. Stanley took no notice of the fact that the two were obviously uneasy. He sipped a goblet of wine and expounded with great delight on the foundation of his postnuclear research center.

"This had been father's winter retreat," he said with a smile. "When the weather got too severe in Oregon, we simply slipped away down here. It has what is now the greatest research facilities in North America. Being a small island, surrounded by jungle terrain that is tougher than any seen on mainland Mexico, we are quite safe.

"The terrain, by the way, was developed by my father, who had something of a green thumb in addition to his many other talents. We haven't had many visitors since the war. Those that do land usually go away discouraged. Those that find this compound . . . well . . . they do not leave it."

Traveler sipped a cup of coffee, preferring to keep what wits he had in reserve about him. "With all your high-tech toys and your obvious knowledge, haven't you ever been tempted to *aid* civilization?" he offered.

Stanley laughed into his wine. "Oh, but I am. I'm keeping it on its toes, you see. The last wave of civilized man went about things the wrong way. It ignored the strengths and weaknesses of the common man and woman, concentrating instead on the strengths and weaknesses of highly technological weapons systems. Eventually those systems became the most important aspect of dozens of governments. The needs of the people fell by the wayside.

"You saw the results in America during the 1980s, during the presidencies of both Reagan and Frayling. More and more tax dollars were poured into weaponry. Absurd weaponry. Weaponry that was doomed to obsolescence as it was actually conceived. Star Wars? Come now. That was an off-the-wall idea at best. Missiles in movable silos, constantly being shuttled to new locations via rail? Straight out of the Keystone Kops.

"Yet, the government persisted in its folly. The results? The haves continued to pursue wealth and the have-nots got less and less. Believe me, if there hadn't been a nuclear war, there would have been tremendous social upheaval in the country. You saw signs of it. A return to racism. Millions of militant homeless roaming the streets. Street crime was up. Drug use soared. Survivalists created massive armed camps in the South and the West."

"But your proposed system of government will be different," Traveler said evenly.

"Of course. Once I bring the current governments to their knees with an army of hunter-seekers, all politicians will be forced to reconsider their current directions and alter them accordingly. The structure of government will have to change. In America people may have to sacrifice some personal freedoms, but in the long run they will benefit from it.

"The hunter-seekers will patrol the borders of all nations, removing the burden of defense from the common man. Mothers will no longer watch their male children become cannon fodder. And all citizens will be educated. Highly educated. Their social status will be dictated by the amount of knowledge they possess, not the amount of toys they accumulate.

"Imagine—nation after nation of scholars inventing, writing, painting . . . delving into fields of knowledge for the pure exhilaration of it."

"And if a few unsuspecting tourists have to be sacrificed right now, it's nothing when compared with the final good your plans for world government will bring," Traveler said with a sigh.

"Exactly." Stanley nodded. "And besides, it's not

like I'm sacrificing them. I'm not tying them to some large stone altar and killing them in front of some pagan god. Everyone here has a sporting chance, although I will admit that you are the first guest who will actually be able to test the hunter-seekers' abilities on a more than routine level."

"What am I supposed to do?"

"Out there," Stanley said, "is a man-made jungle. Before bed this evening I will give you a map of it as well as return your combat knife—we took the liberty of going through your luggage. What the hell, I may as well throw in your pointy little stars too. Shuriken? Before I forget, may I suggest you stay out of the bog? There's quicksand out there that is quite unmerciful, a sort of maxi-quicksand Dad developed. It's almost voracious.

"Excuse me, I'm babbling. This is just too exciting. At dawn tomorrow, armed with the map and your wits, you will be turned loose in the jungle. I will give you a four-hour head start."

"And then release the hunter-seeker?" Traveler said.

"Yes. Yes, indeed. Once released, his purpose will be only to hunt you down and eliminate you. At that point your purpose is to either stay out of his way, which I doubt you can do forever, or kill him, which no one has been able to do as yet."

"How long does this party go on?" Traveler said.

"One day and one night. Twenty-four hours, plus your four-hour head start."

"And if I avoid him?"

"We will pluck you out of the jungle and bring you back."

"And if I kill him?"

"The same promise, although I will want to interrogate you to find out what went wrong with my creation. But *that,* I'm afraid, is speculation that borders on science fiction. The best you can do, I'm afraid, is stay alive until I call him off."

Traveler nodded. He glanced at Michelle. She had a look of total fright on her face. "Look, I don't mind your concepts of the future, all right? Some of them are pretty sound. But as far as my participation in this . . . lark . . ."

"Your participation is necessary for its success."

"I don't want any part of it."

"Your wife will die, as promised."

"Suppose I say yes and fail?"

"She dies as well."

"And if I win?"

"You both get to leave."

Traveler took a sip of coffee. "You expect me to believe that? We could alert the authorities."

"I'll ask you for your word about that. And frankly, even if you go back on your word, you have no idea where you are. There are countless islands off the Mexican coast now. The volcanic activity after the war created dozens. The whole west coastline of North America was boiling over with new land masses. Even if you did try to convince the authorities, I doubt anyone would believe you. Plus, you'll be found so full of heroin that I doubt anyone would take your hallucinations seriously. You see, I do plan things quite well."

"Yeah, you seem to think of everything," Traveler said.

"That's the way I was raised." Stanley shrugged. "Well, are you game?"

"It seems that I *am* the game—" Traveler grimaced —"or the prey, at least."

"You have just the proper touch of sardonic humor." Stanley smiled. "Excellent. Perhaps some of it will rub off on my child."

"You talk about him as if he were human," Traveler said.

"Well, he *is* to a certain extent."

"What is he?" Traveler asked. "Robot? Computer? Cyborg? Mutant?"

"A scientific potpourri." Stanley beamed. "Something that has resulted from no one branch of science but a little of several. Would you like a peek?"

Traveler nodded. "What the hell."

Stanley pushed a button on a small console at the head of the table. An immense wall panel behind him slid open, revealing a six-inch-thick barrier of safety glass. "He can't see you," Stanley said. "Although I'm sure he senses that we are looking at him."

Traveler's jaw dropped open. He heard Michelle gasp. Behind the glass stood a large humanoid figure, some seven feet tall. Covered with smooth, sleek fur, it walked upright. Its legs were taut and athletic. Its arms were long and limber, topped by taloned hands. Its face was something out of a nightmare.

Its ears were pointed, almost lupine. Its snout was similarly long, mouth brimming with teeth. It resembled a humanoid wolf or German shepherd in its bone structure.

Making its hairless face even more nightmarish were its eyes—fiery red, alert. Darting this way and that.

The creature pivoted about in its enclosure, large shackles on its ankles. It sniffed the air curiously before staring deliberately at the glass.

"Ah, the jig is up," Stanley says. "He knows he's being watched now. Well, we can gaze a few moments longer. He's a sullen little boy. He won't perform for us now. He'll simply stare at us resentfully. He likes his privacy, you see."

"What the hell is it?" Traveler said.

"A combination of genetics, biochemistry, and state-of-the-art mechanical technology," Stanley said. "Basically, I created its skeletal system from scratch. Its inner frame is a mass of lightweight metal and plastic, pulled together by the ultimate artificial heart. The rest of him is flesh, though. Synthetic flesh."

"Artificial flesh?"

"Uh-huh. Actually, there were great strides in that area made before the war in burn centers around the world. When a person was horribly burned in the old days, flesh from different healthy parts of his or her body had to be lifted and placed onto the burned area. This practice gradually became obsolete as the practice of growing synthetic patches of skin came into vogue. The skin was perfectly fine. Resilient. Strong. Its only drawback was that it was a bit paler than normal human skin. A tad less attractive.

"Cover it with hair, however, for purely cosmetic purposes, and you have something that looks quite, uh, fearsome, don't you think? Real blood courses through the body, a unique feat, I would say. The blood is that of a human. The beast's sensory apparatus is based on that found in a wolf. Very acute hearing. Wonderful sense of smell. An ability to run that surpasses man. That's where the metal skeletal system comes in handy. No conventional bonework, shaped in a vaguely human assemblage, could keep up with the hunter-seeker's mental commands.

"Which brings me to his brain. Oh, I had fun with that. I assembled it. Nurtured it. Treated it. Taught it. It took me five years to get it where I wanted it to be. Now, with the prototype done, I can crank them out quite easily through genetic cloning, but this brain . . ."

"Basically, it's human but with a difference. I nurtured cellular clusters from three different species of brains—that of the wolf, the mountain lion, and, of course, man."

"Whoa, now," Traveler said. "Those are pretty far afield."

"Yes. Structurally. But cellularly none of us are that far apart. Taking their brain cells, part of their essence, and introducing them into an already functioning brain that had been prepared with a solution based on my father's neurotoxin—"

Traveler blinked. "That *thing* has been treated with the neurotoxin?"

"More than treated, I'm afraid," Stanley said. "My creation thrives on it. You see, part of its skills are derived from the fact that it is always 'on.' Always ready to track subjects down."

"Uh, Doc," Traveler said, "what happens if you produce an army of those things and suddenly they decide, one fine day, to revolt? To turn against their master?"

"Oh, the hunter-seeker is incredibly loyal," Stanley said. "In many ways, he's like a big dog. When I created him I gave him the senses of a hunting animal and the dedication of a human. What I didn't give him too much of, however, was the ability to rationalize, to think, to put his thoughts together in new and possibly independent ways.

"And, as a precaution, if the poor baby doesn't have a small amount of the neuro-stimulator added to his chemical makeup each week, he simply runs down. Turns into a large, shambling, and quite ordinary beastie. Wave bye-bye to your competitior, Mr. Paxton."

Stanley jammed a forefinger into the button and slid the wall back into place.

Traveler shot a glance at Michelle. She looked at him helplessly. Traveler flashed her an easy grin. It was a here's-another-nice-mess-you've-gotten-me-into look. Classic Oliver Hardy.

"If I agree to this Lassie show," Traveler said, "you have to give me your word that nothing will happen to my wife when I'm gone."

"Done," Stanley said. "I apologize for the rough treatment you received en route here, Mrs. Paxton," Stanley said. He turned to Traveler. "Frankly, she put up more of a fight than any of my men expected. One of them will be urinating in quite a unique manner for months to come."

Traveler had to laugh, in spite of the situation. "She was always headstrong."

"Footstrong, too," Michelle muttered.

"Oh, honey," Traveler said. "You never did follow orders well."

"That's what you get for marrying an independent woman, *dear.*" She grinned back.

They touched toes under the table. Traveler found himself grinning at her. She returned the smile. A sudden warmth spread through his body. He felt a lot better now.

"Well," Stanley said, embarrassed at having to interrupt an obviously touching moment, "I would allow you two to spend one last night together but I'm afraid, Mrs. Paxton, that your husband is going to need a good night's sleep if he is to successfully run our gauntlet tomorrow."

He arose from the table. "I will, however, allow you one or two minutes together before my guards lead you to your separate chambers."

He bowed to them both. "Until tomorrow."

Traveler and Michelle stood, watching the man exit the room. Once he was gone, Traveler moved to Michelle's side of the table and, sitting next to her, held her hand.

Michelle was shaking her head, sadly, from side to side. "Looks like this is it."

"On the plus side," Traveler said, "we know what's going on."

She shot him an incredulous look. "You're kidding me."

"Hey, we knew it was risky when we said we'd take the assignment."

"Risky? This is suicide!"

"Thanks for the vote of confidence, *dear.*"

Michelle squeezed his hand. "I'm sorry. I know you're an old hand at survival, but there's no way you can survive out there with that . . . that . . . thing."

"Why not? I was weaned on the same brain juice."

"What?"

"The neurotoxin I was dosed with is the same stuff that boy lives for."

Michelle put her hand to her lips and began gnawing on her fingernails. "I don't know if I can watch you go through this."

"You won't have to," Traveler said with a smile. "I'm sure Stanley will give you a play-by-play description in your room if you request it."

He put his arm around her. "Look. Bottom line is—this is something I have to do. If I refuse, we're both dead. All I have to do is stay alive for twenty-four hours and I buy us a ticket out of here. Stanley still thinks we're Mr. and Mrs. All-American. It's not that big a deal. Twenty-four hours. I've stayed alive twenty-four years since the Nuke-Out. What's another day?"

Michelle turned to him and hugged him. "Thanks."

"For what?"

"For making me feel better."

Traveler stroked the back of her neck with his left hand. "No big deal."

She gently pushed herself away from his chest and stared deep into his eyes. "You know what I regret?"

"Not being able to play the accordion?"

She laughed. "How did you know I couldn't play?"

"You'd have bruises on your chest."

She slapped the back of his hand. "I'm sorry we didn't use the magic fingers together," she blurted.

Three guards came into the room. They motioned to Michelle. She nodded and walked toward the door.

"Hey," Traveler said, being led out by an additional two guards, "there's always the night after tomorrow. I still have plenty of quarters."

He heard her laughing behind him as he was led

from the banquet hall. The sound of her laughter, the smell of her perfume that still hovered about him, filled him with a deep sense of emotional peace. He was glad she was feeling better. He was glad she was less afraid.

Personally, he was scared out of his wits.

He had no idea how he'd stay alive out in that jungle twenty-four minutes, let alone twenty-four hours.

12

Traveler stood on the deck of Stanley's jungle home as the first signs of daylight appeared over the trees. Headband tied securely across his forehead, shuriken wristband attached to his right wrist, combat knife strapped to his side, and map of the jungle grasped in his hand, he stared at the vast expanse of steaming green terrain before him.

Stanley handed him a canteen. "There's food to go with this if you'd like."

Traveler shook his head no. "It would only slow me down."

Stanley's boyish face positively shone. "Excellent attitude. A man of nature. I like that."

Two guards brought Michelle out of the compound. It didn't look like she'd slept all night. Neither had he, actually, but he was used to sleepless nights. His head had throbbed during the night, making it impossible for him to sleep. He resisted popping any aspirin or painkillers. He didn't want to dull his senses. Perhaps even pain could spur him on. He was facing an impossible task, he knew that. He'd need every sense he could muster. Even pain. Perhaps pain most of all.

He had used the time to study the map of the jungle. He hadn't been pleased by what he had seen.

He flashed her a confident smile. "Hello, wife."

She returned his smile weakly. "Sleep well?"

"Like a log," he said.

"Well," Stanley said, looking at his Cartier wristwatch, "time is slipping by."

Traveler nodded. He walked up to Michelle and hugged her. She returned his embrace, breaking it only to give him a short, tender kiss.

Traveler flushed slightly. There was real emotion behind that. Somehow, in this time of danger, their roles as partners, agents, had blurred, been transformed into something else, something more, something human.

Something touching.

He kissed her on the forehead before leaping off the balcony. He ran into the jungle, stopping once to take one last look at the compound. Stanley stood, like a child transfixed, giggling as the first rays of sunlight hit the trees. Tears ran down Michelle's cheeks.

Traveler sighed and ran full tilt into the thick underbrush. It was damp beneath his feet. A reptilian mist curled around his legs as he plunged onward. Awakening birds called out from all around him. Their cries seemed mournful, painful to his ears this dawn.

Countless, nameless insects chirped, burped, and twittered from positions beyond his vision. Soon the vegetation grew too thick for him to run through. Pulling out his combat knife, he used it the best he could as a machete.

His mind whirled as he slogged onward. He was rusty when it came to guerrilla warfare. For the last two decades he had been well armed. Well equipped. Even when he had to come up with makeshift weaponry, he had the basics around him. Gunpowder. Plastique. Bullets.

He had none of that now. There would be no incendiary bombs, no bouncing Bettys, no homemade rockets or grenades. There would be just the damp earth beneath his feet, the trees all around him, the dank, humid sky above, and a man-made killing machine at his back.

He sliced through the bushes, cursing himself. He was tired of being backed into corners. Yesterday he had been told something he had been hoping to hear for months. He wasn't dying of cancer. He was going to live. Punch line? He'd probably be slaughtered by a maniacal, genetic nightmare.

He continued to push onward. His mind went into overdrive. He suddenly recollected the feeling of Michelle's lips on his. They had been warm. Soft. Moist. They had rekindled in him feelings he thought were long dead.

He smiled bitterly as the knife's blade met the vines and the oversized leaves.

Damn her. She had made him miss things he had never actually experienced. Things that had been denied him. Pieces that had been missing.

He checked his map and then glanced at the sky.

Judging from the angle of the sun, he would be in quicksand territory soon.

He would have to do a lot of planning in the next day. He simply couldn't outrun the creature. He would have to manufacture ways to slow the creature down, cripple it, kill it if he was lucky.

He paused at the edge of a stagnant pool of green scum, taking a sip of water from his canteen.

His head suddenly spun. He recapped his canteen and replaced it at his side. The hair on the back of his neck began to arch. He shook all over. The neurotoxin in his brain caused every fiber of his body to quiver.

He plunged wildly into the dark jungle before him, in a near panic.

He knew exactly what his brain was telling his body.

Stanley had gone back on his word.

He had no four-hour lead time at all.

A deafening roar sliced through the jungle.

Traveler stopped dead in his tracks, sweat pouring down his forehead.

He clutched the knife in his hand and sliced at the foliage before him, trembling.

The beast was loose.

13

Its roar made the jungle tremble, the birds scatter, the monkeys flee. It tilted its massive head up toward the sunlight. The rays warmed its snout. It stood for a moment at the edge of the forestland, taking in the air, the light, the smells. It felt the damp earth beneath its feet. *This* is what it had been created for.

It was part of this. It was part of nature. The beast squatted for a moment, rubbing its ankles with its immense paws. The chains had rubbed a circular patch of hair off both legs. It felt the red skin tenderly. It had no idea why it was kept tethered inside the structure for so many days at a time. It did not strike the beast as being correct, somehow.

It had been created for the outdoors. Why keep it away from its place in the world?

The beast bellowed one more time and set off on a leisurely pace through the jungle. It would prolong the hunt as long as possible. It had no great desire to capture its prey, kill it, and then bring it back to the compound to be rewarded with another week of prison.

The human would offer little or no challenge, it knew that. None of the others had before this one. In truth, it was growing tired of the weekly hunts. At first, in its infancy, it had been an amusing game, but now there was a sameness about it. The relentless exhilaration it had once felt had long ago faded. The beast could not understand what pleasure its human creator derived from witnessing such a mismatched game of wits. The humans never had a chance. They were not part of nature. They were animals, true, but animals so divorced from the natural order of things that they might as well have been machines.

The beast lumbered through the forest, enjoying the scents and smells. There were things in its mind it did not fully comprehend, a clash of feelings, of emotions. It had first begun to feel them four hunts ago.

After returning its prey to the white-robed one that day, it watched the white-robed man and his workers torture and kill the female human. They had eaten and imbibed while the female was stripped and battered. Several of the men had copulated with her before. They had eventually discharged a weapon into the back of her head.

The creature was puzzled over the ritual. There was nothing natural about the act, nothing just. The creature realized it was still in its infancy, still growing, but it was old enough to know what was necessary and what was not in order to survive. This act struck him as being cruel, subanimal somehow. The female human had not been given the chance to survive. She had been butchered. In the jungle there was no butchery without a cause. Animals did not kill other animals for pleasure.

The beast sat at the side of a stagnant pond. It sniffed the air leisurely. Its prey had stopped here recently. The creature extended a hand into the stagnant pond, causing ripples. A dragonfly buzzed by. The beast watched the sunlight glimmer against the insect's wings, causing tiny kaleidoscopic shimmers of color. It watched the ripples in the pond. It would pursue its prey at its leisure. There was no hurry.

It glanced at its reflection in the pond. An alien pang echoed in its chest. It was not natural, what it did. This hunt. This test. Why pursue an inferior species for sport. Sport was something unknown to it yet something it understood. There was a visciousness connected to it in its brain . . . the human part of its brain.

The beast stared at its overgrown paws. Crude. Misshapen. That of a human but yet nonhuman. The howl slipped out of its throat before it could stop it. It was beginning to realize something about itself.

The beast was not natural. The beast was an abomination. It was something that had been thrust into nature, had not evolved from it. That thought filled it with sadness. It was the only one of its kind, doomed to be solitary forever.

The creature stuck its muzzle down into the pond. So many strange feelings, so many new thoughts. It lapped the stagnant water. The smell made its nostrils flare. In spite of its alien origins, the beast felt it was good to be alive in this world. The jungle had become its home.

It sat up abruptly. The human was near. It sniffed the air, catching not only the scent of its prey but, for the first time, understanding the *emotion* of this human. The beast cocked its head inquisitively. It had never experienced that sensation before. Certainly it had picked up on the fear of its previous prey, but there was something *more* to this man.

The beast slowly arose. The hair on the back of its neck slowly arched. There was fear in the air, to be sure. But there were other feelings too. This man was determined to live. The drive was strong and solid, not scattered and frantic. The beast was impressed. It slowly walked forward, sniffing, registering the scents. More than scents, really. It was picking up its prey's emotional makeup. Its essence. Its prey was breathing in the spirit of life. The human was keeping his fear in check.

The beast concentrated, somehow extending its mental range further and further. It glimpsed feelings of loneliness, weariness, anger, resentment, determination emanating from the diminutive mortal.

The beast was shocked. This prey was certainly more complex than the others. As it walked it tripped against a large rock, sending the small boulder tumbling in front of it. The rock had gone some three yards before it struck something on the path. A branch flew upward. A vine, in the shape of a lariat, ensnared the rock and attempted to send it hurtling up to the top of a tall tree.

The beast watched, astonished, as the vine clung to the rock. A trap. The human had set a trap for the beast. The creature roared, both in anger and glee. It felt pleasure seeing the vine noose. It excited him to think that a human would show that much cunning. It was almost animalistic. Commendable, really.

The beast paused for a moment, considering its options. It could plunge full force into this contest or dawdle, allowing the human to build up its self-confidence before the beast closed in for the kill.

The beast reasoned that, no matter how much cunning the human possessed, it would not be enough. Humanity had distanced itself too far from the world of nature to try to run back into its bosom now. Nature would reject the human. Nature would make him weak, make him feel the burden of his years of civilization.

The beast would finish off the human easily. Somehow that thought saddened it. This man, this prey deserved a better fate than that. The beast whimpered, thinking that the female human at the white-robed one's dwelling deserved a better fate as well.

It sat on its haunches, regarding the trap before it. The sun was shining brightly. A warm wind wafted through the underbrush. Birds were singing nearby. The beast would continue the hunt. Later. It took in the world around it, a warm feeling filling its chest.

Right now there were more important things to experience.

14

Traveler had heard the trap snap to life. He heard the beast roar. He smiled to himself. Maybe this wouldn't be as difficult a task as he had envisioned after all. If he had ensnared the thing, he could easily kill it with his combat knife while the animal dangled upside down from a very, very high tree.

He ran toward the trap, expecting the creature to be bellowing with rage. Silence. He slowed his pace. Carefully peering over a large boulder, his heart plummeted. The trap had been sprung, all right, lassoing a large rock. The beast sat on its haunches before the hastily rigged guerrilla device. It seemed to be examining it, perhaps meditating on it.

Traveler cursed himself and ran farther into the jungle. He wasn't at all sure of his prowess at jungle fighting. Worse yet, he wasn't at all sure how intelligent this creature was. It was no ordinary animal, to be sure, but it didn't possess the logic of a human.

At least Traveler hoped it didn't.

He had this nagging thought in the back of his mind, a puzzling thought. If the beast was so cunning, so swift, so relentless, why wasn't it pursuing him now? Surely, in spite of all of Traveler's efforts, the creature could easily pick up the scent of one lone human in a dense jungle.

A sudden bolt of panic seared through Traveler's brain. Suppose the creature was toying with him? Suppose the beast was giving Traveler enough rope to hang himself?

He discarded the thought almost as fast as it had occurred to him. No animal could do that. No animal he was aware of, anyway. But suppose this creature was *more* than an animal. Its brain, after all, did have a human basis.

Traveler came to a point in the jungle where a clearly cut trail funneled into a narrow point. He began digging furiously, first with his knife and then with his hands.

It was growing late in the day now. The sun would be disappearing within a few hours. At night he would be helpless. The beast would have the advantage in terms of smell, hearing, and sight. But if he could slow it down before then, cripple it . . .

He stopped digging when the pit was five feet deep. Taking several shafts of bamboo, he quickly sharpened them into spearlike instruments before planting them firmly into the bottom of the pit. He then carefully cut some light branches and placed them, crisscross style, over the mouth of the pit. He sprinkled grass and debris on top of them and, finally, covered the grass with a healthy layer of dirt.

He walked up to the pit and then leapt over it, making sure his scent would be all over the earth on the trail. If the creature sprinted down the trail, following the scent, it would be in for a surprise when it hit the twig trap and then the punji sticks at the bottom of the pit.

With the creature's weight, Traveler was sure that a fall into the pit would severely hamper its running ability. The punji sticks would plunge into it, tearing up through its feet and, hopefully, clear through its legs. It would bleed profusely. If Traveler was lucky, the beast would never get away from the spot alive.

Traveler continued to trot through the jungle. He paused for a moment, taking a sip of water from his canteen. He wasn't comfortable relying on luck, relying on one crudely constructed line of defense. Just in case the pit only disabled the monster, he began cutting more vines from the trees around him.

Perhaps the tiger-trap routine hadn't worked the first time, but if he rigged one up in tandem with two or three more spring-released booby traps, he might be able to inflict a lethal blow.

Traveler worked furiously, slicing the leaves off the vines, wrapping them, knotting them, pulling down the strongest, most resilient branches of nearby trees into a crazy-quilt design.

Sweat poured from under his headband. He tasted the bitter salt drops on his sun-baked lips.

The seconds turned to minutes, the minutes to what seemed like hours. Traveler continued to knot, to tie, to pull. Finally, when he was finished, he trotted off.

He was going to survive, damn it.

He was going to live. And if he lived, he had to be hard, he had to be cruel, he had to be as mean-spirited as his adversary. He had but one goal now, one thought spinning around and around in his mind.

The beast must die.

15

The beast snored on the bank of a small pond as the afternoon sun began to lower. It stirred lazily as a bird called out above him. The beast raised its eyes. In its mind it named it the "ow bird." The bird seemed to be screeching "ow, ow, ow," over and over again.

The beast yawned, feeling the warmth of the sun on its shaggy body. Slowly it got to its feet. Soon the sun would be setting. It supposed it would close in for the final confrontation after dark. The human would be frightened then, surrounded by strange sounds, alien terrain, the shadowy unknown. In truth, the creature would be sad to dispatch the human, not only because it was a senseless act but because the beast would once again be cast into its cell following its glorious victory.

It tried to sort out its feelings toward the white-robed one. He was the beast's master. The beast's creator. But somehow the beast instinctively knew that white-robe wasn't its god. The beast stared at the cumulous clouds wafting overhead. Its god was somewhere out here. Its real creator was all around it, just beyond its grip.

The creature's thoughts went back to the white-robed one. If this man was so concerned for the beast's welfare, why didn't it set the beast free? Why did he allow the beast's mind to nearly fragment before injecting it with another needle filled with life's blood? Week after week. So many questions. So many new thoughts.

The beast slowly walked through the jungle. Something was happening to its mind. It was beginning to reason. Over the past four hunts, more and more strange, complex images were troubling it. Perhaps this was the way with all animals as they matured, but the beast doubted this. It had no capacity for speech, so there was no way it could communicate with white-robe, no way it could express what it felt.

Perhaps that was just as well. It sensed that white-robe had not created the beast for intelligence. The beast realized that it had been created for one purpose and one purpose only—to kill. That had been all right at first. During its childhood everything had been important to the beast, everything it did filled it with pleasure. But now it felt that it was outgrowing its primary function. It was beginning to sort out what was essential to it and what was not. The beast was sure that white-robe would be shocked if he knew how much the beast could fathom, and how many of white-robe's teachings it had already dismissed as trivial.

The beast suddenly grew angry, envisioning white-robe laughing as the beast brought back each successive kill. The creator, so small, so weak, so human. The creation, so large, so powerful, more complex than white-robe imagined. Losing its temper, the beast smashed a mighty fist into the trunk of a tree, splintering it.

Why had it been put on this earth? Surely it had to have some other function than simply to kill. Death is easy. Living is not. The beast raised a taloned hand to its forehead. When its mind strayed into this territory of reason, the different factions of its brain seemed to clash. The animal side of it grew furious, frustrated. The human side wished to pursue the train of thought, come up with a solution. This was all so new. Six, seven hunts ago, the beast was quite satisfied to tear its victims to shreds for the reward of white-robe's soothing tones and a few pounds of raw meat. But the soothing tones irritated it now. The meat made its stomach turn.

The beast loped off down a narrow trail. It picked up the scent of the human again. More than that, it picked up on the human's thoughts. Thoughts, not just feelings. Not just emotions. That was new. For one brief instant it had a vision of the man as he had once been long, long ago. A boy. A little human. Living in a house with larger humans. The picture faded as quickly as it had appeared.

The beast paused, suddenly aware of some strange link between the pursued and the pursuer. It had never encountered that before. The beast grew suspicious. Something was wrong on this hunt. There was an alien factor, something decidedly out of control.

The beast walked down the path warily. It sniffed the path, eyes darting back and forth for some sign of ambush. This human was a crafty one. He made the beast apprehensive. Another new emotion.

The beast watched the path grow narrow. It continued to move forward. The path grew narrower still. The beast stopped. Something was odd about this scent. It was constant, fulsome, directly in front of it. The creature raised its snout. The wind was blowing toward it. The man's scent was also prevalent some five yards in the distance. But there was a gap. A point where the scent was almost nonexistent.

The creature stared at the path. Footprints. Footprints. No footprints. Footprints again. The beast purred. The human was indeed clever, but not clever enough. The beast tore a large limb off a tree and tossed it in front of it. The limb hit the earth with a crash. The beast watched, fascinated, as the limb disappeared beneath the earth, swallowed up whole. A small flurry of sticks and earth crashed down with it into a hole.

The beast walked forward and peered down into the pit. It saw a dozen pointed branches angled up in its direction. The beast roared with outrage. This puny human was out to kill the beast. The man was trying in earnest now to deal a fatal blow. The beast roared and roared again. What did this man know of the beast? Why did this man wish to see it dead? It was an infant still. Growing. Learning.

The beast suddenly stopped howling. A thought occurred to it. What did the beast know of this man? Why did the beast wish to hunt him down and slay him? Because of white-robe? Because that was the purpose the beast was created for? The beast blinked. White-robe had lowered an animal to the tawdry level of a human.

The futility of the hunt suddenly overwhelmed the beast. It gnashed its teeth, tossing its human side away. The animal in it came to the fore. It ran its tongue over its razor-sharp incisors. It would be good to taste human blood again. This would be the finest kill of all.

It would not let go of that thought. It could not let go of that thought. Its survival depended upon that.

16

Traveler ran blindly through the forest, slashing, hacking, stabbing madly at anything in his path. The only sounds that reverberated in his ears were those of his own heartbeat, his panting, wheezing, his feet crashing into the underbrush.

Suddenly a sharp pain sliced through his forehead. He tumbled head over heels onto the forest floor.

The sun was setting, filling the forest with an eerie orange glow. He blinked. Suddenly everything before him was gone.

He was peering into the punji-stick pit. Anger. Resentment. Rage filled his heart.

He blinked again.

The forestland once again stretched before him. Instantly he realized what had happened. Somehow he had viewed that pit, not from his perspective, but the perspective of the beast. His mind reeled at the thought.

He had experienced such an event only once before. It had been shortly after he and his three comrades had been dosed with the neurotoxin in El Hiagura. For one brief instant he had experienced the scene, not only through his eyes, but the eyes of Hill, Orwell, and Margolin.

He slowly staggered to his feet, aware of what was happening. Somehow the neurotoxin in his brain and the neurotoxin in the brain of the creature were reaching out, communicating in some strange way.

His heart thumped wildly at the thought. Something inside of him was changing, altering. Was he regressing? Was he mutating? He began to sweat. If he could see through the eyes of the beast, then surely, before long, the beast would be able to see through his eyes as well.

The thought unnerved him. If that was so, then soon, very soon, he would have no place left to hide. The beast would be able to track him through Traveler's own perceptions. There would be no defensive trick, no trap that Traveler could devise that the beast would not be aware of.

He cursed himself. He clenched his fist. Before he knew quite what was happening, he felt a strange sound well up from within him. Facing the setting sun, he took a deep breath and bellowed at the jungle around him. Roared at the orange sun. Screamed at the stars beginning to show themselves in the gradually darkening sky.

He panicked. He realized that he had to act soon. He had to confront the beast. Maim it. Kill it. Destroy it forever. It was something he was not looking forward to because, in a very real way, he and the beast were linked in a manner he dared not acknowledge. They were kindred souls. Man-made killing machines, both currently doing what they knew the best.

He staggered forward, knowing that the confrontation was inevitable. A sudden wave of fear engulfed his senses.

He wasn't afraid to die.

That wasn't it.

He was afraid of what killing the beast would do to his own soul . . . to what was left of his own humanity.

He thought of Michelle. The fear that had been on her face when he left the compound. He thought of their kiss. The warmth of her lips. He choked back a sob, remembering Roberta and the love that was denied him. He thought of little Kiel, incinerated in a holocaust that robbed the boy of his youth.

Wiping a stray tear from his eye, he uttered a hoarse cry and ran forward. Ran without logic. The animal within him roared in his mind. He galloped through the jungle, eyes wide, slashing out wantonly at the foliage in his path. He smashed. He cut. He tore. He ducked. He dodged. He darted. He went where logic, human intelligence, and the battered map tucked in his belt warned him not to go.

When his feet hit the bog he realized he had made a mistake. He tried to pump his feet up and down, frantically attempting to escape. Soon he was up to his knees in the stuff. Abruptly he stopped struggling. He glanced down at the swirling, bubbling muck beneath his body.

He was slowly sinking in it.

Quicksand.

He glanced about, trying to spot some way out of this mess.

He managed to laugh at his predicament.

Think like an animal . . . die like an animal.

17

The beast bounded through the jungle, angry, resentful. Things were changing too quickly. It was feeling uncomfortable. This human was a formidable opponent. As it sprinted forward it glanced this way and that, attempting to spot any snares in the making.

Darkness would be falling soon. Darkness would place it at a distinct advantage. The human would make an easy prey then. The beast would snuff it out.

A sudden picture entered its brain. The beast thought of the woman at the compound and the sad, fearful look on her face as it entered the jungle. It smelled the scent of her skin. Felt the touch of her lips as they pressed against its own. When the beast was dead, the woman would be killed.

The beast stopped suddenly, shaking its regal mane from side to side. No. That wasn't right. It wasn't the beast the woman had kissed. It wasn't the beast the woman was concerned about. It was the human.

The beast whimpered. Its mind was being invaded. Invaded by the thoughts of the human.

The creature slogged onward as picture after picture slammed into its mind's eye. For a time it was in another jungle, a jungle of long ago. It was one of four humans struggling under the effects of a deadly substance in the air. The substance that now gave its brain life.

Waves of fear and helplessness washed through the creature as it frantically continued its forward march. Its mind would not let up. It saw a woman and a child standing in a compound of some sort. A sudden flash. A roar. They didn't have time to cry out. Their skin began to burn. Their blood evaporated. Soon their skeletons were nothing more than ash, mingling in the breeze with the ashes of countless others.

The creature cringed, attempting to ward off the telepathic blows. It saw cities go up in whirlwinds of flame. It witnessed women and children slaughtered by humans wielding guns from the backs of motorcycles. It felt the pain of solitude. The bitterness of a future lost.

The creature tried to will its consciousness to dwindle. It was no use. Picture after picture assaulted it.

The monster roared and continued on its way, tearing and ripping wildly at the forestland around it, mangling leaves and trees with its taloned hands.

It paid no attention to where it was going.

It didn't notice the way the vines before it were twisted in such a strange manner.

It heard the swish before it felt the vine snap around

its left ankle. Abruptly the creature found itself being pulled high into the air, propelled by a strong tree limb. The beast roared as the vine pulled it higher and higher.

It heard the snapping of other vines. Twisting and turning, upside down some ten feet off the ground, the beast saw the large tree limbs head for its torso. It raised its massive forearms in front of its head, attempting to ward off the blows.

A tree limb, breaking it in two at impact, crashed into its left arm but drew no blood. The beast wriggled as it was hit by another. And another. And another.

Soon the hissing noises stop.

The wind seem to die down.

The jungle was silent.

The beast dangled from its trap. It could free itself. It was confident of that. All it had to do was pull itself up and slash the vine with one of its taloned hands. Not yet, though. It had to gather its strength.

It was very, very tired.

It was drowning in waves of another being's emotions.

The beast blinked its eyes at the ground below it. The ground vanished. It saw the woman and the child again, peering out from behind the flames engulfing their compound. The beast was seized in the grip of emptiness. Something snapped within it and it found itself doing something it had never done before in its short lifetime.

It felt a small drop of water exit from its eye. A second drop dribbled forth as well. A shortness of breath racked its chest. The beast felt the tears run up over its eyes and onto its forehead. It watched them cascade onto the jungle floor below its twirling head.

It surrendered to the sadness. It wept for the future denied it, for the family it would never have, for the human it would never be.

Sobs tore through its chest. It found itself tormented by the thought that, although the most powerful creature on the island, it was powerless when it came to its future. It had been programmed to kill. It had been designed to be special. Now the creature cursed its hunter's instincts, despised its uniqueness.

It considered the fact that within an hour it would have to snuff out the life of a human that was somehow educating the creature, sharing with it.

Granted, the human out there was not educating the beast intentionally. Still, it was exposing the creature to more honest knowledge, more insights, than the white-robed one had ever intended.

The beast sighed.

The world was closing in on it.

It was losing its childhood. Maturing. Becoming an adult of its solitary species. Its prey was responsible for that. The beast owed the human a debt of gratitude.

The beast blinked its eyes and was suddenly faced with a scene of dank, humid horror. The bog. The human was caught in the bog. The picture was brief, fleeting.

The beast relaxed somewhat. There was some humor to all this. The beast was trapped in the snare of man. The man was trapped in the snare of nature.

The beast slowly arched its back and swung up,

grabbing the vine with two hands. It began slashing the vine with one, long talon.

The difference between the man and the beast, however, was that the beast would easily disengage itself from this feeble trap. The man could not escape the forces of nature.

18

Dr. Stanlcy sat on his back deck, staring out into the darkness. Howls. Cries. Roars. That was all he had heard. And no sign of his creation as yet. He didn't like that. He didn't like that at all.

A bell chimed behind him. He stood and walked into the dining room. Michelle was already seated.

"The condemned gets one last meal?" she asked.

Stanley sat at the end of the table. One of his minions began serving dinner.

"Your husband is resourceful." He said, toying with his food. "No one has ever eluded the hunter-seeker this long."

"You don't seem pleased," Michelle said.

"On the contrary, it is the ultimate test." He smiled halfheartedly. He pushed his food aside and lit up a cigar.

"That's bad for your health," Michelle said, enjoying seeing the madman ill at ease.

Stanley nodded curtly. "A small vice I allow myself. Cuban cigars. My father had connections in the government. A lost art, smoking. A pleasure that should not be denied."

"Whatever turns you on," Michelle said, scooping up a forkful of mashed potatoes.

Stanley glared at her. Michelle suddenly felt a surge of optimism. "So, if Kiel returns tomorrow, ahead of your critter, we get safe passage?"

Stanley blew against the tip of his cigar, causing it to glow a bright red. He slowly left his place at the head of the table and walked behind Michelle.

"Do you know the sense of pain a lit cigar can cause when placed on one's nipple?"

Michelle stiffened. "I've never had the pleasure."

"I could begin torturing you tonight, you know," Stanley said.

"Why?"

"As you said, whatever turns me on."

"You enjoy sadism, I suppose. It goes with your territory." She glanced at the cigar. "Is that what you have planned for me? Torture? Rape?"

Stanley placed a clammy hand on her shoulder. "Indeed. Although I don't participate myself."

"You like to watch," Michelle said.

"Yes, indeed I do. Conventional sex pales alongside my more creative endeavors. But several of my associates do enjoy *fondling* my female guests before I bid them a final farewell."

Stanley smiled. "It's amazing what five men can do to a woman in, let's say, thirty minutes. Sometimes they take turns with our guests. Perhaps a trio begins. When they're done, two more of my associates partake of pleasure. On occasion I've seen them descend, five at once, on a lovely lady.

"The mind boggles at such a scene, I know, but it is possible for all five to insert themselves in various orifices at once. Of course when that happens they sometimes have to suspend their partner on certain devices, but as long as they're happy . . ."

He took a drag off the cigar and blew the smoke onto Michelle's neck. "And after they're done they amuse themselves for a little while longer. They have these devices that, under normal circumstances, would be considered quite harmless. But when creatively applied . . . a flicker of flame here, a small dose of electricity there, a thin blade applied to white skin . . . Well, let me tell you, it makes very enjoyable viewing for me. Quite stimulating. Quite entertaining."

Michelle placed her fork in the mashed potatoes a second time. "And if my husband returns alive and well?"

"Then he'll get to watch as well."

"You never did intend to let us go, did you?"

"My dear, you are so naive. A very enjoyable quality."

"Why not kill me now?"

"I don't like to rush into things," Stanley replied, walking back to his place at the head of the table. "One has to plan one's life. In the days of chaos following the war, I discovered that, in order to avoid total insanity, one had to make up rules. Adhere to a routine. The essence of sanity, Mrs. Paxton, lies in routine."

Michelle placed the fork on her plate. She didn't consider Dr. Stanley a fine example of sanity.

Stanley puffed away at his cigar. "Were I to let my men have you now, it would rob me of my entertainment tomorrow. I like watching my men in the daylight. You can see so much more."

Michelle glanced over her shoulder. One of the three mountainous men from Arrowhead was leering at her. She glanced at the hot tip of the cigar. She felt her nipples harden.

Stanley tilted his head back and laughed softly.

Michelle pushed the plate of food away from her. She wasn't all that hungry anymore.

19

Traveler stared at the stars twinkling above him. The bog glistened in the light of the bright, fall moon. The stuff was up to his waist now. He tried to calm himself. Back in the days when the neurotoxin really tore into his system, he had perfected a zen exercise combining breath control with mental prowess. He had to disassociate himself from the panic.

He had to distance himself. Reach into each part of his body and relax it. He envisioned his muscles as being tense and then soothed them. He saw his body as being heavy. He coaxed it into buoyancy. He had been breathing deeply, slowly for almost a half hour now. He erased the image of the beast from his mind. He scraped the painful memories of the past from his consciousness.

You are flesh and blood, he told himself. A product of the natural world. The world you are part of now is of the same origins. From earth you were born, into earth you will return. But not quite yet, thank you.

He slowly scanned the surrounding forestland. He realized there was no way he could reach out and grab on to the nearest vine. They were beyond his reach. He was yards away from the nearest tree limb. He would not allow himself to struggle, to flail about in the muck. That would surely lead to his doom.

A brightly colored bird, a small parrot, perhaps, stared at him impassively from a tree. For a moment Traveler imagined himself to be as free as that bird. If only he had wings, he could simply flap them and remove himself not only from the bog but also from the island.

The bird squawked, as if uttering a mocking laugh, and flew off, allowing Traveler to return to reality.

All right, Traveler reasoned, the bird may have the flying power but he had the brain power. It was time to put it to the test. Logically, there had to be a way out of this. He wasn't some dinosaur struggling in a tar pit, doomed to extinction because of his massive body and tiny mind. Hopefully, he was a bit beyond that in terms of evolution.

He stared at a small tree, no more than a sapling, standing at the edge of the bog.

A small smile broke across his mud-spattered lips.

If he could bend that tree somehow, get it nearer to his hands, he was sure he could slowly, effortlessly, pull himself free. But how?

His knife was lying on solid ground some five feet away. There was no way he could hurl it. His breath began to quicken. His heart began to pound. Calm yourself, he ordered. Calm yourself.

He glanced at his right hand. The wrist containing four ninja shuriken was above the level of the bog. He stared at the tree. It would be tricky. He would have to slice into the tree without severing its trunk. He would have to get the tree to bend, not topple.

Traveler slowly withdrew a shuriken with his left hand. He stared at the base of the sapling. Using his wrist, as opposed to his entire arm, he hurled the tiny metal star at the tree. The shuriken zipped clear past the tree, embedding itself in a nearby hedge.

Traveler fought the panic. One down, three to go. He carefully slid the second shuriken out of its container. Taking careful aim, he sent it spiraling toward the sapling. The second shuriken sheared off a small branch and sent it tumbling down into the quicksand.

Traveler breathed deeply. Concentrate. Accent the positive. He removed a third shuriken and glared at the base of the sapling. He fingered the shuriken with his left hand before sending it slicing through the night air.

The shuriken smacked into the base of the sapling, neatly passing through half of its base. It landed with a thump on a mound of dirt behind it.

Traveler watched the tree shimmy. He wasn't sure if it would fall at all. It might not be heavy enough. The breeze might blow it in another direction. That was another possibility to consider.

Traveler held his breath and waited. Slowly the tree began to tilt in his direction. The rubbery trunk gradually descended toward the bog. Traveler allowed it to land atop the mire before he made a move to grab it.

He extended his left hand around the tip of the sapling. Taking a deep breath, forcing every ounce of air he could into his lungs, he tried to make his body as buoyant as possible. Raising his right hand, he grabbed on to the tree firmly. He slowly pulled himself toward the edge of the bog. Hand over hand. Slow breath after slow breath.

He prayed the sapling would hold his weight.

He closed his eyes, willing his heart to maintain a steady rhythm, commanding his breathing to avoid panic.

Hand over hand, inch by inch, he pulled himself toward solid ground. Five feet more. Four feet more. Three . . . Finally the tree could take no more. It snapped off at its base. Traveler, acting quickly, extended a hand and dug into the solid earth next to the tree.

Exhaling, he quickly lifted himself out of the mire and onto the damp jungle floor. He staggered to his feet and retrieved his shuriken.

Traveler collapsed for a moment on the dank ground. His body convulsed. He was cold. The jungle was rapidly losing the moist, oppressive heat of the day. A small breezed wafted through the trees, causing the wet grime on his body to tingle, to chill him to the bone. His teeth began to chatter. He leapt unsteadily to his feet. He was not about to show weakness now. He had no time.

Grabbing his dagger, he sheathed it and pulled the soggy map from his belt. Holding the parchment up toward the moon, he stared at the layout of the jungle.

He could feel the presence of the beast approaching.

It was nearly time for the final showdown.

Traveler scanned the map frantically. Finally he

found what he was looking for. A lake. Fresh water, probably. Pocketing the map and unsheathing his knife, he began slashing through the jungle once again.

Toward the lake.

Toward his salvation.

20

The beast stumbled to a halt at the edge of the bog. It sniffed the air warily. The human had been here, all right, but now he had gone. Why hadn't the beast sensed that? It concentrated on honing in, with empathy, on the prey. It was impossible, now, for it to connect with the man. The beast wondered why. Why were these alien thoughts suddenly being shielded? How were they being kept from the creature?

It crouched at the bog's end. It could see the displacement in the slime where the body had been. It gingerly picked up the sapling from the mire, sniffed at it. A human smell. But more. A sense of determination. Of calm.

The creature purred. Its prey was beginning to show traces of true animal instinct. This struck the creature as being both admirable and fearful. If this man, this human, could adapt to the ways of the jungle, then perhaps he would be able to outsmart the beast.

The creature crunched the sapling to a pulp in one of its oversized hands. Going back to the white-robed one didn't matter now. Now, the hunt was all important. The creature had been tricked, had been weakened, had been caught off guard. That had never happened before.

Its mind had been altered, its senses twisted. The beast tossed the remains of the sapling down. The time had come to end this game once and for all.

Somehow, winning the contest struck the creature as a matter of pride. It was not about to be bested by a creature physically stronger and mentally weaker, than itself.

Slowly, carefully, it stalked through the green landscape. The moon was bright overhead. It silently followed the tracks. It sniffed the tree limbs torn asunder by the man's knife. The human had a plan, it was clear. He was veering from the well-trodden paths of the jungle, embarking on a crazy-quilt course that sliced through the deepest, darkest part of the forest.

The creature realized that it was a trap of some sort. No, more like an invitation. Here is where I'll make my stand, the human was declaring. Here is where we'll meet.

Fine, the creature thought. Fine. We will see who is mightier. We will see who is more powerful. The creature stopped its march, again attempting to hone in on the feelings of the man. They were nowhere to be found.

It punched its way through a densely overgrown area of the land. The human had it easier than the beast. He was lower to the ground than the creature. He surely found it easier to dart through the jungle. That thought angered the animal. The beast tossed aside tree limbs with ease. The bruise on its arms made by the human's traps caused it small amounts of pain.

Its ankle, already worn raw by the shackles imposed by the white-robed one, was bleeding from the vine lariat.

The pain gave the beast a renewed sense of energy.

The creature stormed onward, totally focused. One goal in mind. To destroy before it could be destroyed. It came to a clearing. Before it stretched a small, shimmering lake. The beast could tell from the shape of the lake, the lingering smells on it, that it had been man-made. Nothing this pristine could exist in such a dark, forboding terrain.

It paused at the shoreline, gazing at the lake, impressed by its beauty. It snorted to itself. This was not the time to be swayed by emotion. It glanced about its large, taloned feet. The human had obliterated most of his tracks, but he couldn't erase his smell.

The beast slowly circled the lake, following the human's scent. It stopped tracking at a spot densely overgrown. The scent was all around it. The human was hiding here somewhere. The creature attempted mental contact. The feelings of the human eluded it.

The human was getting cagey. Obviously it was more advanced than the beast in censoring its emotional output. No matter, the human may have been better versed in terms of treachery and deception, but it was *still* a stranger in this primordial environment. A stranger who had overstayed his welcome.

A small rippling on the lake caught the creature's eye. At the shallowest part of the lake, the section nearest the shore, a lone reed stuck up from the water. The beast nodded to itself. It had found its prey. A human could not stay underwater indefinitely unless it fashioned some sort of breathing apparatus to suck in the precious air it needed. A hollow reed would do that well.

The beast stifled its first instinct, to roar in triumph. Not yet. Not quite yet. Slowly, in a feline manner, it crept up to the edge of the lake. Glancing about it, it saw a large boulder. Picking up the massive stone with both hands, the beast held it high above the reed.

Emitting a deafening roar, it sent the boulder crashing down into the water on top of the spot where the human lay, hiding. The beast stood at the water's edge for a second. In that second it was assailed by an avalanche of contradictory emotions.

It felt triumph, to be sure. It had the best of the human. But it also felt remorse, shame. It had killed the only teacher, the only honest human, it had ever encountered. It had, once again, fallen into the behavioral trap that the white-robed one had designed for it. The beast had learned so much today, yet it had been bested, in the end, by its overwhelming desire for bloodlust.

The creature shook its head clear of the thoughts. It was a hunter. It had hunted well. Now it was time to retrieve its trophy.

The beast then plunged into the lake, yanking the reed from the water. No air bubbles emerged. Puzzled, the beast reached down into the water, trying desperately to locate the body of the human. It located the rock. It felt silt. It didn't feel anything remotely fleshy.

The creature stiffened.

The back of its head exploded in pain.

It felt itself losing consciousness.

The back of its head pained it a second time. It cried out helplessly as it felt its logic leaving its body. The creature lost its balance and fell backward onto the shore, a look of shock on its face.

21

Traveler had watched the beast approach the lakeside from behind a large clump of shrubbery. He held a huge tree limb in his hands, gripping it the way a child would a Louisville slugger. He had made sure that his scent was all over the area. He had rolled in the dirt. Climbed up trees. Leapt in and out of the lake. The beast would not be able to pinpoint his scent now. He was sure of it.

He watched the creature puzzle over the all-encompassing smell of human flesh. He watched it move to the edge of the lake with the grace of a Brobdingnagian ballet star. The creature spotted the reed, as Traveler had hoped. It was one of the oldest tricks in guerrilla warfare. Hopefully, though, the creature was not well versed in the ways of guerrilla fighting.

The beast eyed the reed. It seemed to chuckle to itself. Traveler watched the creature pick up a large boulder and slam it down into the lake. Traveler winced, thinking of what would have happened to him if he *had* decided to hide beneath the lake's surface. He fought back his fear. He couldn't allow his feelings to show.

When the beast pawed the lake, seeking the body of its prey, Traveler ran forward, limb in hand. Taking a full swing, he connected with the back of the creature's head. The beast let out a yelp of surprise and then stiffened. It was too stunned to react, too surprised to fight back.

Traveler swung a second time, slamming the limb into the base of the monster's skull. The beast began to teeter. It toppled backward onto the shore, landing at Traveler's feet.

It was out cold.

Traveler stood above the creature.

The moon shone down on the mighty hunter-seeker's face. A small trickle of blood dribbled from its moist muzzle. Traveler stared, panting, into the visage of this man-made monster. So this is the next generation of superweapon, he thought. This is the creature powerful enough to cause governments to crumble. One more blow to the head and the monster's brains would be splattered for yards around.

Traveler gripped the club. The monster whimpered, sounding more like a frightened dog than a killing machine. Traveler hesitated. This beast wasn't responsible for its actions. A power-crazed man had created it. A man had programmed it. A man had perverted all that was natural in the animal kingdom, thrusting an animal's God-given instincts into a direction bent on wanton killing.

Traveler sighed. He had to kill it. His own life was at stake. Michelle's life. The lives of countless humans to come. His hands sweated around the club.

The creature stirred beneath him. Its reddened eyes began to flutter. The creature exhaled. It was a sigh of resignation. The monster suddenly looked weary, broken. Something had robbed it of its strength. Something more than Traveler's club.

Its body shivered slightly, the wind drying the pellets of water trickling down off its fur.

Traveler noticed how strong the beast's body was, how perfectly it was designed. The fur was sleek and smooth. The legs taut and well muscled. Yet, for all its natural beauty, for all its innocence in the ways of man, it was still an enemy. An enemy to be destroyed.

The creature opened its eyes wide and stared directly at Traveler. Traveler gazed into those bloodshot orbs intently. The monster stopped shivering. Traveler felt his hands grip the club tighter. The beast did not take his eyes away from Traveler, staring so deep that the mercenary felt his heart surge.

Traveler was unable to break eye contact. In spite of everything, there was a bond between them. Two creatures, one of a kind, facing extinction in a rapidly changing world. Traveler shook himself free of those thoughts.

The creature continued to gaze into Traveler's eyes. It wasn't a gaze of contempt, or hatred, or fear. It was a look filled with sadness, of recognition.

Traveler took a deep breath.

The creature stared deep into the man's heart.

Traveler heard a word buzz through his brain, a word unspoken but felt nonetheless. He had not thought it. It was a thought from somewhere outside his body. A message sent. The word reverberated through Traveler's consciousness again.

"Brother."

The creature whined softly as Traveler raised the club one final time.

22

The first rays of morning light peeked over the trees of the jungle as Stanley stepped out onto his back deck, cigar in one hand, coffee in the other. He frowned at the daybreak. The hunter-seeker should have been back by now. It was impossible for the creature to fail. It had the speed. The strength. The weight. The cunning. No mere man could stand a chance against the beast, neurotoxin or no neurotoxin.

He hadn't intended it to be a fair fight, just more of a challenge for the creature.

He turned his back on the brightening paradise outside his compound and stalked into the dining hall. He sat, angrily, at the head of the table as Michelle was shoved into the room by two thugs.

"Good morning," she said sarcastically. "Any word from the critter?"

"No," he replied sullenly. "And no word of your husband, either."

"So it's a draw?"

"Hardly," he said, almost flicking the ash from his cigar into the coffee cup.

"If neither returns by noon, I will allow my men to start their games for my amusement."

An alarm sounded in the compound. One of the pretty boys from Arrowhead ran in. "Sir? We have a visitor."

"Don't bother me—"

"From the jungle?"

Stanley tensed. The door to the room burst open. Traveler stood there, exhausted but grinning. His pants were spattered with dry bits of muck. His torso was scratched and bleeding from his stay in the bush. His face was sunburned and bruised. He took his knife and casually removed a leech from his forearm. "Hungry little sucker," he said, casually.

"You have no idea the number of nasty little beasties you have out there," Traveler said, crushing the leech under his shoe. "Why there are mosquitoes out there as big as bluebirds. And the snakes . . . well, it wasn't at all a pleasant experience, Doc."

He flashed a smile at Michelle. "Hi, honey."

All color had drained from Stanley's face.

"Great," Traveler said, sitting next to a beaming Michelle. "I'm in time for breakfast. I sure worked up an appetite out there."

"Th-the hunter-seeker?" Stanley began.

"Oh, your big hairy guy?" Traveler said, taking a slice of toast from Michelle's plate. "He couldn't make it."

Stanley began to simmer. "Is that all you have to say?"

"Nope." Traveler smiled. "Jam?"

"What?"

"There's only butter here for the toast, do you have any jam?"

Stanley stood, shaking. "What have you done with the creature?"

"Nothing that he wouldn't have done to me," Traveler said, chewing his toast slowly for effect. "Now, after breakfast my wife and I would like to clean up and get out of your playland here."

"You must be joking."

Traveler stopped chewing. "Do I look like I'm kidding around, Doctor? The toast is burned. You might want to try to hire better help out here. Service isn't all it's cracked up to be. From the outside, this place looks like a four-star kind of place but . . . the butter's soft too. Anyhow, I assume you'll be giving us clean clothes as a bon voyage present. If I remember correctly, your men did a number on the outfits we were wearing at the casino."

"Mr. Paxton, surely you can't be as naive as your wife! I mean, I can understand *her* believing that you'd be let free, but you? A mercenary? A veteran of how many wars and battles? I find that very disappointing."

Michelle was shaking now. Traveler nudged her knee with his. Traveler sighed, finishing his toast. "Yeah, well, you're pretty disappointing to me as well, Stanley. I keep on hoping that I'm going to run into people with some sense of honor, you know? People who put a value on their word. But time and time again, I'm disappointed."

Stanley puffed on his cigar. "You have my sympathies."

"Thanks," Traveler said, standing. He was immediately surrounded by the three burly goons from Arrowhead. They held pistols. The pretty boy at the door clutched a Uzi.

"You know," Traveler said, smiling, "last night it occurred to me that you might not want to keep your word. Call me a cynic. I don't know. And then, when I thought about that, I began thinking, now if this anemic little asshole is going to weasel out of his deal, what the hell am I doing out here hunting down a creature that I have no cause to dislike, let alone hate enough to kill? When you consider the situation in those terms, you wind up getting involved in quite an existential problem."

"Spare me," Stanley said. "Would you like to be tortured first or would you like to see your wife mutilated?"

"What the hell, I might as well go first. I mean, it's the gentlemanly thing to do, right? Chivalry and all that. But, please, before Larry, Moe, and Curly here get too fancy with their pistols, let me finish my story. I'm getting to the really good part here."

"By all means."

"So, here I am, in the middle of the jungle, cogitating up a storm. I have to survive. I know that. I have to rescue Michelle from your slimy hands. So, bearing that in mind, I try to figure out just how can I come back here and deal with a madman such as yourself in a way that can convince you to let us go."

"There's no way you can convince me to let you go."

Traveler grinned. "Nope. I didn't think so. So, I brought along a buddy to add a little weight to my argument."

Stanley blinked. He didn't understand. The room was suddenly shaken by a deafening roar. The closed door behind the pretty boy burst in, pinning the Uzi-holding thug to the floor. There, outside the door, was the hunter-seeker. The creature leapt onto the door, now lying flat on the floor. Traveler and Michelle heard the pretty boy screech as his body was crushed to a pulp.

Even Traveler winced, seeing small bits of bone and hunks of flesh come spurting out from beneath the fallen portal. Something slid across the room, spinning wildly like a top. It was a human hand.

The creature stood atop the door, immobile. Its nose twitched, sensing the feelings in the room. Friendship. Fear. Outrage.

Stanley stood, immobile, at the head of the table. His jaw flopped up and down. No words emerged.

The three thugs at Traveler's side turned as one to face the beast. They hesitated in firing, looking first to Stanley for instructions. After all, it was his creation.

The beast appraised the situation. Its newfound brother was in danger. The evil humans, the ones who had done the killings of the females, were threatening his friend with firearms. Something clicked deep within the beast. The beast simply would not let any harm come to his only equal.

The creature sprang to action, slashing out with his taloned claws. The three goons made a move to scream in unison. Their voices never made it up from their throats to their mouths.

Michelle stifled a scream as their three, newly disembodied heads tumbled onto the table and rolled slowly toward Stanley. Their bodies, spurting geysers of blood from their opened necks, tumbled onto the floor, twitching.

"What have you done to it?" Stanley demanded. "What have you done to my hunter-seeker?"

Traveler stood, hugging Michelle. The beast stood behind him. "Not a thing," Traveler said. "It's what you've done to it."

"I created it!" Stanley declared.

"True enough," Traveler stated. "So, in a twisted way, that makes you its parent. I was a father once. I didn't get to see my kid grow. I never got the chance to see my boy through adolescence, but I had been prepared for it. You see, my dad gave me good advice about fathering when I was still in grammar school. I wanted to be a pirate back then. I think I chose that occupation just to piss off my pop. He didn't get pissed off, though. He told me, 'Son, when you're old enough, if that's what you want to do, go do it.' In other words, Doc, he knew when to let go."

"I don't see how you can equate your lowly preadolescent years with this masterful scientific creation that you've somehow perverted!" Stanley said, in a voice that sounded like a macaw on speed.

"The deal is, you created the beast but you don't own it. This animal's evolving. Maturing. It can reason, Doc. Surprised? Part of its brain is human, after all, and you've dosed him enough with that stuff your father used on me to kick its conscience forward. It can *feel.* It can *think.* It has emotions. It's not just the killing machine you envisioned. It's matured way beyond that point. In fact, I wouldn't doubt if it didn't need that weekly injection of brain booster anymore. I think what you see before you is a totally whole being."

"Impossible. It's an animal, nothing more," Stanley declared.

"We're all animals," Traveler said. "Some of us are just more evolved than others."

Traveler ushered Michelle toward the door. "Where are you going?" Stanley shrieked.

"We're leaving. We're going home. And if you have any brains, you'll let the hunter-seeker go home too."

He pointed to the jungle. "Out there. That's where it belongs, not chained in some lab."

Stanley rushed forward, grabbing one of his slain thugs' handguns. "You're not going anywhere," Stanley said, his eyes wild in fright. "And my creation is going right back into the lab. If you've distorted its perceptions, I can realter them. Bring it back to its more primitive ways."

"I don't think so," Traveler said. "And I'd watch who you're threatening. Our friend here can understand every word you say."

"Rubbish," Stanley said, leveling the gun at Michelle and Traveler. "Tonight the hunter-seeker will enjoy the pleasure of having raw meat. Raw meat stripped from your bodies after I've taken care of you."

"Don't say you weren't warned," Traveler said, glancing at the creature. The creature emitted an ear-splitting howl and, extending its right hand, placed it firmly over Stanley's head. Stanley pivoted his body, trying to shoot the creature where it stood. He hadn't the time to aim. The creature gave Stanley's head one brief twist. In a moment Stanley wasn't struggling anymore. The beast allowed the body to fall onto the floor.

Michelle was in a state of shock. Traveler patted her arm. "It's okay. The hunter-seeker and I had a meeting of the minds last night."

He slowly walked up to the creature. The creature stared at the body of Stanley, a mournful expression in its eyes. The white-robed one, the one who had given it life, was dead. He had killed its own parent-human.

Traveler seemed to sense the feelings of the creature. "He wouldn't have changed," Traveler said softly. "He would have tried to own you, to keep you as nothing more than a weapon. That isn't your place. That isn't your function."

The beast turned toward the rear deck. The jungle stood outside, lush and green, steaming with morning mist. Traveler walked with it. "That's your place. Out there. Live your life in harmony with the world around you, brother."

The creature nodded. Traveler gazed up at the beast. "You're the only one of your kind. You will be lonely at times. But there are ways you can communicate with the others out there that people haven't conceived of. Perhaps, in time, you will be less lonely. Perhaps there are things you can bring to that world."

The creature put a protective arm around Traveler. Abruptly it roared and, crashing through the picture windows separating itself from the jungle, it galloped off into the underbrush . . . and freedom.

Traveler turned and walked toward Michelle. "I don't believe what I just saw," she stammered.

"Why not? We hunter-seekers have to stick together." Traveler faced the window and watched the beast disappear from view. "Good luck, brother," he whispered.

Michelle stood next to him. "What happened out there?"

"I guess you might say we had a jungle classroom experience." He smiled. "Every once in a while we forget that we're all guests on this planet and man was one of the last guests to arrive. Yet, we have the audacity to try to reshape the world, use it as our tool."

He sighed. "There's a natural order to things, you know? And no matter how many governments, how many big brains, try to scramble that order, eventually nature survives. When the creature and I were out in the jungle, we became part of the jungle. And as guests of that environment, we realized that hunting each other, killing each other, just wasn't natural in that context."

He glanced around the room. "This whole place, a colossal waste of intelligence. Just another exercise in egomania."

The smell of the jungle filled the dining area. "Well," he muttered, "maybe not. Maybe the beast will kick off a new evolutionary leap. Who knows?"

He put his arm through hers. "Are you up for a boat trip out of here?"

"Am I ever."

"Good. The harbor is just outside the front of the compound. I spotted it coming in."

"Let's go. I'm still shaking."

"One moment," Traveler said, picking up the Uzi from the body of the squashed pretty boy. "I have a little cleaning up to do."

Michelle followed Traveler into Stanley's master lab. Traveler gazed at the machinery, the vials, the tissue cultures and opened up on them with the Uzi. Glass shattered. Bits of fleshy matter dripped onto the floor. Walls erupted into waves of concrete flakes and bits of mortar.

"Good enough," Traveler said, "I'd torch the place, but if there's any more of that neurotoxin around in great quantities, that would only send the stuff drifting off over the jungle. And right now I don't think the world is ready for birds that can do calculus."

"Should we try to find it and bring it back?"

"No," Traveler said. "If it's here, Jefferson can send a few men down to pick it up in a month or so. I don't think anyone will be moving here for a while to play with that stuff. They'd have a hell of a time commuting and, besides, with a neighbor like the beast . . ."

Michelle stifled a laugh. "You are weird, you know that?"

Traveler placed an arm around her waist. "True, but I always keep my word, right? I said I'd be back."

"You did."

"And I'm here."

The two walked toward the boat basin, arms linked. "Jesus," Michelle said suddenly, "I can't imagine Jefferson's face when he reads our report."

"I'm not sure he can read," Traveler said, stepping onto a small outboard craft. "Orwell may have to digest this . . . and I know Orwell loves science fiction."

23

Traveler guided the rented Subaru away from Long Beach Harbor and headed toward the freeway. "What'll you do now?" Michelle asked.

"Retire from the CIA as gracefully as possible."

"Then what?"

"I thought I'd head back to Bay City. It's nice there. Plenty of sun. Plenty of ocean."

"Sounds peaceful."

"Yeah. I could go for a little peacefulness right about now. How about you?"

"Me?" Michelle stammered. "Well, after we file the reports, I guess I'll go back to work at the Agency. Wait for my next assignment."

"Suppose I pulled a few strings?" Traveler asked. "Got you a low-level assignment in Southern California?"

"The Bay City area?"

"As a matter of fact, yes."

Michelle hugged his arm. "Sounds peaceful."

"Shit!"

Traveler swerved the car to avoid a bus speeding in the opposite direction, zigzagging in and out of the oncoming lanes. "Someone's in a hurry."

The bus continued to veer wildly. Michelle stared at the vehicle, its taillights flashing.

"Look, there are children on board."

Traveler peered into the bus. Boys and girls, aged about eleven, were at the windows, crying, terrified. Their hands were tied together.

"That doesn't look like a school picnic to me," Traveler said, kicking the car into a screaming U-turn.

The Subaru pursued the speeding bus. "If that sonofabitch doesn't slow down, he's going to run off the shoulder," Traveler muttered.

The bus swung dizzily to the right of the road, kicking up a shower of dirt and grit. Its right rear tire left the macadam and sliced into an embankment of soft earth. Before long it was mired in the silt, surrounded by dust. The driver continued to gun the gas, causing the large vehicle's engine to roar and its right rear tire to spin madly. A wave of dirt and silt whined into the air, cascading down onto the highway.

Traveler slowed the car down and exited. "Wait here," he told Michelle.

The bus driver scrambled out of the bus. "Damn," he exclaimed.

"Doesn't look too bad," Traveler said to the surprised driver. "You can probably rock this old baby out of the dirt."

"Yeah," the driver said, recognizing Traveler. "I guess I could, friend."

"Friend," Traveler said, laughing at the kid he had rescued from a lynch mob only a few days before. He glanced in the bus. The children were all securely tied to the seat backs in front of them. They were crying. "Out on a trip?"

"Yeah," the young man with the doe eyes said nervously. "Taking some sick kids to a hospital. It's not much of a high-paying job but, you know, I like the work. It's a real community-service sort of thing."

Traveler nodded. The young man was sweating now. Traveler glanced at the rear tire. "You were in a real hurry there."

"Well, I promised to have them there by sundown. They need all this complicated medication. The staff is there, just waiting for us to arrive. I have to keep my word, right?"

"Yeah," Traveler said. "We all have to keep our word."

He pulled out his Colt and fired once, hitting the boy square in the forehead. The driver collapsed on the pavement, like so many dirty rags tossed in a heap. Traveler walked over to the boy's body. There was no need to fire a second shot.

"Some people learn that the hard way," he muttered.

Traveler walked back to the car. "You up for driving a bus?"

"Sure," she said. "But the driver . . . I don't understand. You just—"

"The punk from the town we passed through. The

one everyone said was a child-snatcher? Turned out they were right."

"But you saved him before," she said, staring past Traveler at the driver's body lying sprawled on the highway.

Traveler shrugged. "His parole was conditional. He just broke the rules. His parole just got revoked."

He turned and walked toward the bus. "Come on, let's cut those kids free and calm them down."

Traveler and Michelle entered the bus. "Hello, boys and girls," Traveler said. "Now, I want you all to just relax. The bad man isn't going to hurt you anymore. We're all going back home to your moms and dads."

The children stared at him silently, not believing it as yet.

"My name is Kiel and this is Michelle."

Michelle flashed a sincere smile at the children. "We're here to help you get back home."

One little boy stared at them hard. "Are you two married?"

"Yes," Michelle said.

"No," Traveler replied at the same time.

The boys and girls aboard the bus exchanged knowing glances and began to laugh. Bright splashes of red appeared on both Traveler's and Michelle's cheeks.

"Let's just say we're going steady," Traveler said, beginning to cut the children's hands free. "Let's just say we may be together for a long time."

Michelle smiled at the self-proclaimed killer who just couldn't stop helping people.

She stood beside him and began untying the children as well. "That's a very nice thought," she said.

Traveler nodded, not wanting her to see the color on his cheeks.

"Yeah." He nodded. "It is a very nice thought."

He wondered if he really could be satisfied running a hardware store.

He figured he'd find that out soon enough. He continued to slice through the children's bonds. He heard Michelle whisper something to a little girl. The little girl giggled. It struck Traveler that he had never heard a nicer sound.

It was so spontaneous. So real. So natural. For a moment he found himself, emotionally, both in a good place long gone and a better place yet to be.

Soon the children were laughing and talking among themselves. Traveler and Michelle shared in the laughter.

Soon nobody noticed the body of the driver outside the bus.